DEATHLY TEMPERANCE

NETHERWORLD PARANORMAL POLICE DEPARTMENT: BOOK THREE

JOHN P. LOGSDON

CHRISTOPHER P. YOUNG

Published by: Crimson Myth Press (www.CrimsonMyth.com)

Cover art: Audrey Logsdon (www.AudreyLogsdon.com)

Thanks to TEAM ASS!
Advanced Story Squad

This is the first line of readers of the series. Their job is to help me keep things in check and also to make sure I'm not doing anything way off base in the various story locations!

(listed in alphabetical order by first name)

Adam Saunders-Pederick
Bennah Phelps
Debbie Tily
Hal Bass
Helen Suanders-Pederick
Jamie Gray
Jan Gray
John Debnam
Larry Diaz Tushman
Marie McCraney
Mike Helas
Natalie Fallon
Noah Sturdevant
Paulette Kilgore
Penny Campbell-Myhill
Sandee Lloyd
Scott Reid
Tehrene Hart

Thanks to Team DAMN
Demented And Magnificently Naughty

This crew is the second line of readers who get the final draft of the story, report any issues they find, and do their best to inflate my fragile ego.

(listed in alphabetical order by first name)

Adam Goldstein, Allen Stark, Amanda Holden, Amy Robertson, Barbara Henninger, Beth Adams, Bob Topping, Carolyn Fielding, Carolyn Jean Evans, Christopher Ridgway, David Botell, Denise King, Helen Day, Ian Nick Tarry, Jacky Oxley, Jim Stoltz, Jodie Stackowiak, Kathleen Portig, Kevin Frost, Laura Stoddart, Mary Letton, MaryAnn Sims, Megan McBrien, Myles Mary Cohen, Scott Ackermann, Sharon Robb.

CHAPTER 1

*I*t'd been a few weeks since we last heard from Keller, the dickhead of a mage who had been causing a lot of stir lately in the precinct. While I found it hard to believe he was letting the Retrievers catch our breath from the rout he'd given us, he was being eerily quiet.

But life in the Netherworld Paranormal Police Department, or PPD, went on.

There were runners, lawbreakers, and people who had just forgotten to check in. Usually the last bunch were dealt with via a buzz on their tattoo. Sometimes, though, the "I'll get to it later" mentality landed us on their doorstep.

That wasn't the case right now.

My partner, Reaper Payne, an actual reaper who had done something naughty enough to get him sentenced to live one hundred years in our world, and I were assigned to bring back a werewolf living in the Australian Outback. She was purportedly eighty-one years old, hunched over, and not much of a threat. Unfortunately, families of the locals that she'd been feeding on over the last couple of months begged to differ. To them, she was a vicious wolf.

Had it just been Reaper and me dealing with this, all would have been swell. But ever since Keller's goons wiped out a good number of Retrievers, we'd been forced to take on rookies for training in the field.

As Chief Carter had put it: "Piper, you're one of the best Retrievers we've got, and so I'm assigning you to train new rookies." Technically, that was bullshit, because all Retriever units were being assigned fresh cops.

But he was right. I was the best Retriever. I wasn't saying that because I was arrogant. I just knew that I was good at what I do, and numbers didn't lie. I'd had more retrievals in my short tenure than some cops had had in their entire careers. A lot of this came from the fact that I was immortal. When you had no fear of dying, you were far more willing to take risks. Shit still hurt, though, so I was usually careful.

Reaper was still pretty new to the job, but he'd seen a lot in his years while ferrying people from the world to the Vortex. He wasn't a worry to me anymore. He'd proven himself a number of times already.

The two I still found to be a chore were the officers known as Brazen and Kix.

Brazen was a werebear who also happened to be an asshole. He was big, out of shape, had a perpetually messed-up beard, and his clothes were rarely clean. Kix, on the other hand, was a young djinn who was covered in tattoos and always wore a shit-eating grin.

Now, you'd probably bet that I'd be more excited

about serving with a guy like Kix than I would be serving with someone like Brazen.

You'd lose that bet.

I disliked serving with them equally.

Now, don't get me wrong. They *had* demonstrated themselves to be more than competent during our last couple of missions, but they were still green.

That made *me* responsible for them.

I didn't like being a chaperone.

But those were the breaks, and if you griped *too* much at Chief Carter, he could make your life a living hell. Besides, I owed the chief more than I could ever hope to pay back. If it weren't for him, I'd either be strung out on some crazy drugs, in jail, or both.

"What have we got?" I asked Reaper, knowing he was able to spot people in the area using his internal tracking ability. Some people may have thought that was due to his glowing eyes, but it wasn't. He just had that reaper skill. "Is she on your radar, Reap?"

"There is something…" He trailed off and pointed.

As if on cue, an elderly woman stepped out into the open.

Brazen and Kix went for their guns, no doubt itchy to try out those Death Nails I'd made them practice with. But I held out my hand and gave them a look. They put their weapons away with a sigh.

"Mrs. Donaldson?" I called out, taking my badge from my pocket and showing it to her. I slowly approached. "My name is Piper Shaw and I'm from the Netherworld Retrievers unit."

"What's that?" she called back, holding a hand to her ear. "Could you speak up?"

"My name is Piper Shaw," I yelled back. "I'm an officer in the Netherworld Paranormal Police Department. This is my partner, Reaper Payne, and these are a couple of officers-in-training." I didn't bother to give their names. Mrs. Donaldson didn't seem to mind, but Brazen and Kix were frowning at me. "We'd like to ask you a few questions, ma'am."

At first she looked taken aback, but then she slowly nodded and waved us to follow her.

"I was about to go home and put on some tea," she said, "if you'd care to join me."

"Hmmm?" I replied, not expecting that response. "Oh, right. Sure, we'd love to."

"Damn it," hissed Brazen.

He wasn't one who enjoyed socializing and pleasantries.

"*Heads up, Piper,*" Chief Carter said through our internal comms as we slowly followed after Mrs. Donaldson, "*we have a situation going on down here and I need Officers Brazen and Kix back immediately.*"

"*Oh, darn,*" I replied as relief washed over me. "*How will we ever manage without them?*"

Brazen looked quite pleased with being called back.

"Gee," he said aloud, all smiles, "I'm sure I speak for Kix as well when I say that we absolutely hate to have to leave this riveting catch-the-old-woman caper, but duty calls."

Kix grinned as well, though he seemed less enthusiastic about leaving. Unlike Brazen, Kix was fine with doing the mundane and simpler aspects of the job. I'd wager he was incredibly chuffed to be labeled as a Retriever no matter what his actual duties entailed.

"Toodles," Brazen said before pressing his tattoo and disappearing.

"Good luck, guys," Kix said with a shrug before he disappeared.

Reaper and I looked at each other and resumed following the old woman.

CHAPTER 2

*H*er house was more like a small hut, at least from the outside. The inside was cozy and tastefully decorated. It was minimalistic, sure, but I was one who always took functionality over fluff.

"So, what have I done to warrant having a contingency of Retrievers after me?" she asked as she put the kettle on to boil. "I know I'm getting older, but I do believe I still have a number of months remaining before my annual reintegration cycle."

Every supernatural living topside had to go back to the Netherworld on a set schedule in order to go through reintegration. It allowed them to reset their base needs, go through new training techniques, and to remember that being allowed to live topside was a privilege, not a right.

All of this was necessary to protect the normals living in what we called the Overworld.

While the terms made it sound like supers lived underground, that wasn't really the case. They were simply two separate realities that were close enough to be easily traversed, if you knew how.

Supers had learned how.

So why "Overworld" and "topside?" Because when you went through the portal, it felt like you were going up; when you came back, it felt like you were going down. I couldn't say why the engineers had designed it that way. I'd have thought their arrogance would push them in the opposite direction.

Everyone had their own schedule for reintegration. Newer vampires and werewolves, for example, had to return more often due to their innate desire to attack normals. But even they eventually had their return windows relaxed if they could prove themselves capable of resisting temptation.

Mrs. Donaldson was older. She'd been living among normals for a very long time, and so her record showed that she only required trips back to the Netherworld once per year.

But that was only if she was good.

She was not being good.

"You're correct," I said, watching her closely. "You're not due for your normal reintegration cycle for a few months, but there's been a bit of a glitch in your stay up here."

She put her hands on the counter and turned her head to the side, not quite looking back at us.

"Glitch?"

"You've been eating normals," Reaper stated without inflection.

He was so pedantic sometimes.

"Oh," Mrs. Donaldson said with a light chuckle, resuming her tea-making. "That's all?"

Reaper and I glanced at each other, feeling confused.

"That's a violation of your agreement, Mrs. Donaldson," I pointed out. "You have been through numerous reintegrations, so you should be fully aware that you have broken the law."

"Laws are meant to be broken, child," she replied sweetly. "Besides, I've been a werewolf for many more years than you've been alive." She began pouring. "The people I ate were old and dying. It was for their own good." She nodded to herself. "Yes, I'd say I'm doing the community a service by devouring the old and the sick."

The only thing worse than a murderer was one who truly believed that what they were doing was right. Even if she had the consent of those she was feeding on, it would still be against the rules and regulations of the Netherworld-Topside system. It just wasn't allowed.

"Did these people sign a contract that authorized your disposal technique?" asked Reaper.

"That doesn't matter," I told him in a direct connection.

"I know, but I want to understand her motivations."

"Of course not," Mrs. Donaldson giggled. "Where would the fun be in that? Besides, who in their right mind would sign a document that allowed a werewolf to viciously destroy them?"

There were probably a good many people who would sign that document, but none that would fit that "right mind" classification.

Reaper pressed on. "And so you took it upon yourself to determine if their quality of life was low enough to warrant your intervention?"

"Precisely, young man," she replied, bringing over our tea. "They are normals. We are supernaturals. This entire concept of protecting them from us is asinine. One can simply look at the vast differences in strength, speed, stamina, and intellect to know that they are but sheep in comparison."

"Which is precisely why there are rules in place, Mrs. Donaldson," I stated firmly as I took a sip of the tea.

It went down smoothly at first, and then it began to burn.

She'd poisoned us.

Honestly, I don't know why I was surprised at that. I also don't know why both Reaper and I were foolish enough to accept tea from someone who was a perp. My guess was it had to do with her grandmotherly look.

"Wow," I said, wincing, "the poison you put in this tea burns pretty good."

Mrs. Donaldson smiled as though she'd just given us candy on Christmas.

Creepy.

"Don't you worry," she consoled, "the burning will stop and you'll die peacefully." She then wiped her hands on her apron. "I would have preferred not to have killed you, to be honest, but I believe I have a duty to fulfill here and I cannot allow anyone to interfere."

I nodded at her and set the cup down. Reaper put his down as well.

"The thing is," I said as the burning stopped, "we're both immortal. Poison won't kill us."

Her eyes darted back and forth between us for a moment and her shoulders fell.

"Unfortunately," Reaper remarked, "attempted murder of two Retrievers will be tacked on to the charges already against you."

Mrs. Donaldson sighed, slowly unfastened her apron, took it off, folded it, and set it on the kitchen table. Then she dumped out the rest of the water in the kettle, wiped it clean and set it back on the stove.

"It's a shame that the youth of today don't understand the nature of our power over those who are lesser." She continued tidying up, though it seemed like a pointless endeavor. "If you were even half my age, you'd understand."

"Actually," Reaper responded, "I'm a reaper. I've been around for many of your lifetimes, and I've seen the horrible things that all manner of people—normal and super—are willing to do to each other." He tilted his head at her. "Power is no excuse, I'm afraid. What you are doing is wrong, ma'am."

She chewed on her lip and looked away.

I saw her arm twitch an instant before she snagged a small canister from the kitchen counter and threw it on the ground near me and Reaper.

Smoke belched from the thing and stung my eyes.

I jumped to my feet and moved away from the smoke, firing my gun in the general vicinity of where Mrs. Donaldson had been standing.

JOHN P. LOGSDON & CHRISTOPHER P. YOUNG

Reaper moved quickly to me as we both coughed and waved at the smoke.

Finally, it cleared.

There were Death Nails littering the walls, but Mrs. Donaldson was gone.

CHAPTER 3

$\mathcal{W}$e ran outside and saw the outline of a werewolf running off in the distance.

She'd gone full wolf.

"Shit," I said, leveling my gun at her.

I missed.

"Double shit."

"We can transport ahead of her," Reaper reminded me.

Use of the transporters *was* limited, mostly in frequency of use, but Reaper's special tattoo gave him more leniency over things than a standard Retriever. He couldn't just jump from place to place within seconds or anything, but the cool-down period for him was half that of mine. We could jump to and from the Netherworld pretty rapidly, if there was sufficient need, but hopping around topside or even from place to place in the Netherworld wasn't possible. It could actually kill you.

Reaper had even more issues with this than the average super. The portal system could seriously screw him up if he didn't wear a special mala bracelet that had been infused with magical protections. I was a bit jealous of his bracelet, truth be told. Not because I wanted to have the limitation of requiring one to transport around, but rather because I thought it looked cool. I especially enjoyed the two skulls that sat among the rounded beads. While they were no doubt wholly unnecessary, they gave the bracelet a nice, somewhat sinister look.

"Put us in front of her," I commanded. "Not too close, though. I want to have a few seconds to get set before she realizes what's happened."

Reaper nodded as I put my hand on his shoulder. He pulled up his sleeve and began tapping on his tattoo, dragging his finger around in various patterns. The ink lit up briefly behind his manipulations, showing it was registering his commands.

The world faded.

When it came back into view, we were standing directly in the path of an oncoming werewolf.

"Reap!" I shrieked an instant before Mrs. Donaldson's wolfness slammed into me, knocking me flat on my ass.

"Sorry," he said, staggering slightly from the use of his power. "She was apparently moving more quickly than I'd thought."

"Oh, for goodness sakes," Mrs. Donaldson said as she looked into my eyes. "You two are getting on my last nerve."

Then she reared up and began raining down blows.

She was a lot stronger than I'd expected for someone her age, but when a super moved into their advanced form, they were entirely different. A normal woman of eighty years was like a spry Rottweiler on steroids when in wolf mode.

But I was no slouch in the fighting department, and so I defended myself as best I could. I couldn't last forever, though, and Reaper clearly knew that. He loathed to cause permanent damage, if it could be avoided, but he'd obviously found enough balance to slam into the wolf that sat atop my chest.

They both tumbled away, giving me time to get up and pull out my gun.

Reaper jumped to his feet and spun to face the wolf.

Mrs. Donaldson was also up on her feet. She kicked him in the stones. Or at least where his stones should be. Honestly, I had no idea if Reaper was anatomically correct or not. It had never come up in conversation, after all.

He grunted and dropped to his knees, whimpering like a freshly neutered puppy.

Well, that was one mystery solved anyway.

Just as Mrs. Donaldson was preparing to knee my partner in the face, I shot her leg.

She yelped and hit the ground, writhing in pain.

A Death Nail to the torso or head was guaranteed death to any super. It would split apart in rapid succession, sending bits of itself throughout the body. A shot to an extremity or the ass, though, would just hurt like hell. Fortunately, Nails were built to be able to differentiate between normals and supers. If you shot a normal with a Nail, they could still die, of course, but the projectile wouldn't split apart. It'd just go straight through or it'd stop when hitting bone.

As Reaper continued his moaning, I stepped over to Mrs. Donaldson and repeated the Retriever arrest motto.

"Helen Donaldson," I said, pressing the gun against her head just in case she decided to be ornery, "by order of the Netherworld Retrievers, I, Piper Shaw, and my partner, Reaper Payne, hereby place you under arrest, and we shall transport you back to the Netherworld and present you before the Tribunal for sentencing."

She relaxed and groaned heavily.

"Damn it," was all she said.

CHAPTER 4

With Mrs. Donaldson heading off to processing, and both Reaper and I getting a full commission on her retrieval, due to her being brought back alive, we were back to our desks and awaiting the next assignment.

"How are the jewels?" I asked my partner without turning my attention from the screen. "Still sore?"

"Jewels?"

"Your balls, Reap."

"Ah," he replied. "They are fine, thank you."

"Good."

After a moment, he added, "May I ask why you refer to them as jewels?"

"Google it."

Even though Reaper had been living with supers for a number of years, he still missed out on certain bits of slang and other nuances that one could only get through lots of exposure.

"Piper," called out the voice of Chief Carter from his office, "I need you and Reaper in here pronto."

He wasn't one who used the connector when a solid yell would suffice.

Reaper and I walked into his office and found the older man sitting there, red-faced. This wasn't unusual since he was more often irritated than not, but he seemed a little more vexed than usual. Plus, the pink bottle sitting on his desk spelled that his stomach was churning.

"Sit down," he demanded, which sounded funny coming from a man who seriously looked like he could play the part of Santa Claus. "We have a problem."

"What's up, Chief?" I asked, taking a seat.

In response, he spun his screen around and pointed at it.

"We've got riots going on downtown."

By that, he meant in the Netherworld city center. It wasn't uncommon for there to be little fights breaking out down here, seeing that the city center was basically a soup of races who were innately against the existence of each other.

But full-scale riots didn't happen often.

I couldn't recall even a single one in my years living here.

The Netherworld was akin to New York City topside. It was a large place that was full of buildings and people. Those people were from all the supernatural races. Most of the time, they worked together just fine, but now and then...not so much. On the outer edges of the city were the deeper faction areas. This is where you had to be careful. If you were a vampire entering the werebear area, for example, you'd better have completed your last will and testament because you weren't likely to be seen again.

Those who lived in the city center, though, strived to focus on the greater good instead of just worrying about their own kind. Actually, the only way a super could get a permit to go topside was if they'd first spent a number of years working and living in the city center without incident. That's why the topside wasn't completely overrun with supers.

"Any idea what happened?" asked Reaper. Then he glanced at us both. "I'm assuming riots are rare, yes?"

"They are," answered the chief. "Last one I saw of this scale was in the late eighties."

That brought up a red flag.

The prick known as Keller had last been active in the late eighties and early nineties. Maybe he was back for another round of fun?

"Wait," I said, furrowing my brow at the chief, "I'm assuming you're tying Keller to this just like I am, but he's topside, right?"

The chief shrugged. "Doesn't mean he's not still connected down here."

"Plus," Reaper mused, "we still don't know what his full capabilities are. He could be able to travel back and forth, just as we can."

"True," I agreed. "He *did* gain access to the tattoos of a few Retrievers."

Many of them, in fact. Keller had killed a number of PPD officers, which he'd been able to do because someone on his team had figured out how to hack our tattoos and capabilities. Our resident technician, a goblin who went by the name of Pecker, had changed our ink accordingly, but Keller still had had full access for a short time. That may have been long enough for him to find a way back into the Netherworld.

"Anyway," the chief said, "that's why I called back Brazen and Kix. I've got two officers going to each of the main factions to see if they can figure out what started everything."

Even though Brazen and Kix were training to be Retrievers, they didn't have their stripes yet. They were still full-fledged Netherworld cops, though, which meant it was more important for them to be here than with me and Reaper. The Netherworld was their normal beat. They knew it far better than I did. Hell, if I ever got in my head to leave the Retriever unit and become a beat cop in the Netherworld, I'd probably be apprenticing to those two idiots.

"That's risky," I said, recalling that Brazen was a werebear and Kix was a djinn. "They're not the same race, you know?"

"Of course I know," he replied as if I were stupid. "But they've got the law on their side, and everyone has warrants."

Factions were tough and ruthless, but they weren't stupid. Killing a cop or even roughing one up would result in serious repercussions. Hate only took you so far before logic overruled stupidity. At least that's what I'd learned over my years as a cop. Still, there were times where hate ruled no matter what.

"Have they reported back?" I asked.

"Not yet," he replied, taking a sip from his pink bottle

of stomach soother, "but everyone's just received their final briefing and their assignments. We should hear back within the hour."

"Chief," Reaper said, sounding tentative, "these riots aren't near the Diamond District, are they?"

"They're moving that way slowly," the chief replied. "Why do you ask?"

"Agnes," I answered for him.

"Yes," he agreed.

Reaper Payne, the former reaper who, again, was in charge of taking souls—or whatever you want to call them—from dead bodies and ferrying them to the Vortex...had a pet turtle named Agnes.

Supposedly, this was to help him better understand feelings and emotions. It seemed to have had an impact, too, as he *did* appear to greatly care about that turtle.

"Well," the chief said, notably *not* making fun of Reaper for having such a pet, "you may want to check up on her, just in case."

"Agreed," stated Reaper while getting to his feet. He looked at me. "Do you want to join me?"

"To check on a turtle?" I scoffed.

"Correct."

There wasn't much in the way of sarcastic interpretation when it came to Reaper.

I glanced at the chief hopefully. "Is there *anything* we can do to help with the riots, Chief?"

"No," he said flatly. "We only have so many Retrievers left and I can't afford any of you being injured or killed." He held up a hand. "I know you're both immortal, Piper, but that doesn't mean you can't be taken and locked

21

away. If anything blows up topside, I'll need you for that."

That was a fair statement.

Keller may or may not be pulling the strings down here, but if he suddenly decided to start being a dick again in the Overworld, it'd be all hands on deck.

"All right," I said, pushing myself to my feet and motioning for Reaper to lead the way. "Let's go check on Agnes."

CHAPTER 5

*R*eaper's condo was posh. His eye for decoration had floored me the first time I'd been here. There was white leather furniture, a widescreen TV hanging on the wall, a sound system that could probably piss off the neighbors if Reaper cranked it past two, and artwork that had to have cost him a pretty penny.

In a nutshell, it was no wonder Reaper was doing all he could to condition me *not* to kill all our perps. He needed full commissions in order to pay for all this shit.

Whenever we brought back a perp alive, we got paid in full. If we brought them back dead, or brought back a piece of whatever was left of them, we only got half pay. I could survive on half pay, but that was because I didn't live in the Diamond District. There was no point. I spent most of my time working or at the precinct, so why spend cash on splendors like Reaper did?

Another look around told me that if I had a place like this, I'd probably spend less time at the office.

After a few minutes of what sounded like cooing, Reaper emerged from his room, holding Agnes.

She was a red-eared slider. While I had no idea what that meant in the grand scheme of turtledom, the name appropriately described the red lines on the sides of her head.

"Say, 'hello,' Agnes," Reaper said encouragingly.

"Uh...hello," I mumbled while looking at the turtle.

"I was speaking to Agnes, Piper."

"Ah, right."

I'd nearly forgotten that Reaper was able to talk to his turtle. At least that's what he claimed. Obviously, I couldn't verify this other than to say Reaper didn't seem to be bat-shit crazy. Then again, he said he could talk to his turtle.

I lifted an eyebrow at him but said nothing.

"She said that there hasn't been any noise in the area, aside from the people upstairs." He looked up at me. "They exercise at odd hours, and they're very enthusiastic about it. Lot's of moaning and groaning, and they yell out to various deities a lot."

It was difficult not to laugh.

"Okay," I said with a cough. "Well, it looks like all is good here, so we should probably head on back."

Reaper nodded in agreement and motioned me toward the door.

I glanced down at Agnes.

"What about her?"

"I'm bringing her with me," he said as though he were a child who wasn't about to leave his beloved pet behind.

"It's not safe to leave her here, Piper. At least not until the rioting has passed."

"I see." I didn't, but I wasn't really a pet-person. "Where are you going to put her?"

"I have a special pocket she likes," he replied, opening his trench coat to show me. "We go on little trips all the time."

"Right." I shrugged and headed toward the door and stopped. "A tortoise pocket."

"She's a turtle, not a tortoise."

"What's the difference?" I asked, suddenly wishing I hadn't.

"They're both reptiles," Reaper explained, "from the order of Testudines, but tortoises dwell on land while turtles are either aquatic or semi-aquatic." He looked excited to be having this discussion. That made one of us. "I have books that go into much more detail, if you're interested?"

I blinked at him.

"Uh, not really," I said, and then pointed at the turtle as a memory struck. "Hey, wait, don't those things carry salmonella?"

Reaper balked and looked down at Agnes with a shocked face.

"Agnes!" he whispered sternly. "That's not nice."

While I was still on the fence regarding whether or not Reaper was actually able to communicate with his turtle, there *was* something about the way the little creature was eyeing me that said she *had* said something.

"What did she say?" I asked with a bit of effort.

"Nothing," Reaper replied. "She merely spoke out of

turn." He then wagged his finger at her. "Yes, you did, Agnes. That was rude." He stopped wagging his finger. "Well, yes, I know that, but you have to remember that *she* doesn't know any better."

"Am I the 'she' in that statement, Reap?" I ventured.

"Yes."

I crossed my arms and began tapping my foot. Now, I knew Reaper was a reaper, but apparently even he became uncomfortable when a woman crossed her arms and tapped her foot. The next step was hand-on-hip, which I *knew* he would avoid at all costs.

"What did she say, Reap?"

"Honestly, it's not really—"

"What did she say?" I pressed, moving my hand to my hip. It was inevitable. "Tell me."

He sighed, looking back and forth between me and the turtle.

Agnes kept her head tilted slightly while staring at me with a judging eye. It was like she was mocking me. I knew I could easily squash that damn turtle, but there was something about her that gave me pause. Probably the biggest 'something' was that she could talk to Reaper.

"She said, 'Your mom has salmonella.'"

CHAPTER 6

The streets were relatively quiet as we began moving back to the tubes. We could technically just portal back to the station, but with everything that was going on in the area, we'd been asked to keep the portals to emergency-use only.

"It doesn't appear to be bad here," Reaper echoed my thoughts. "Hopefully it stays that way."

"Agreed," I said, keeping a roving eye on the area. "You never know when the shit will hit the fan, though."

"Yet another metaphor that has never made sense to me," Reaper sighed.

We'd gotten about halfway to the tubes when I sensed something was wrong. There was a stillness in the air.

I stopped and put my head on a swivel.

"Do you feel that, Reap?" I asked.

"Yes."

Good, so I wasn't crazy. I had a tendency of knowing when bad things were afoot, but it was nice to have a second opinion to confirm my feelings.

"Agnes feels it too," he added.

That interrupted my pattern for a moment as I glanced at him while furrowing my brow.

"Swell," I moaned.

Turning my attention back to scanning, I saw someone who looked out of place.

She was a fae and she was wearing a baseball cap. Fae did *not* tend to wear anything that would hide their beauty. They were exceedingly vain people, after all.

Now, it could have just been that she was one of those few who touted how beauty didn't matter.

I'd found that there were only two types of people who said that sort of thing. Really good-looking ones and really not-so-good-looking ones. But the really good-looking ones wouldn't give up their looks for a million bucks, and the really not-so-good-looking ones would pay a billion bucks to be really good-looking.

In other words, that hat gave me pause.

"There's something you don't see every day," I remarked with a nod toward the fae.

"It is odd that she is wearing a hat," Reaper acknowledged. "Fae do not tend to cover up." Then he pursed his lips. "It could be that she is vegan as well."

I wasn't sure how wearing a hat and being a vegan connected in Reaper's head.

"Huh?"

He looked over at me. "I've just found that those who are vegans tend to be less focused on outward beauty."

"They do?"

I was obviously not well-versed in the way of the vegan. It seemed to me that healthy eating and avoidance of devouring animals was just one facet of a person. How that tied into a fae wearing a hat was a mystery to me. Then again, I did have a few acquaintances who were vegan and they *did* seem to carry a particular scent around with them.

Just as I was about to shrug off the fae-in-the-hat as me being too sensitive to the fact that rioting was nearby, she dropped to a knee for a moment, and then got back up and walked briskly away.

"Did you see that?"

"Maybe she was just tying her shoe?" Reaper replied. Then he opened his coat slightly and glanced in the pocket where he was keeping his turtle. "What was that, Agnes? Get down? Why should we—"

I dived at Reaper, knocking him on his ass just as a wave of energy flew over us.

"Ouch," he said, looking up at me. "Agnes also says, 'ouch.'"

All of a sudden, there were screams and yelling in the area.

I pushed up from Reaper and turned around to see that people were tearing into each other. I didn't know what was in the device that the fae had clearly put on the ground, and I had no clue how Agnes could sense something was wrong, but the rioting had begun.

"Why did you tackle me?" Reaper asked as he brushed his coat.

"Ask your fucking turtle," I answered while shoving him toward the tubes. "We have to get the hell out of here."

That was going to be easier said than done because we

were the only two people in the area who had no support. I didn't mean PPD officers, either. I meant neither of us fit in down here. I was a normal, mostly, and Reaper was a reaper. We didn't have vampires to back us up, or werewolves, or pixies, or whatever. We were outliers, and if we didn't get out of here quickly, we were fucked.

Too late.

We'd been sniffed out.

Damn wolves.

"Run!" I bellowed before taking off at full speed toward the tubes.

Getting in there wouldn't save our asses, but if we could get on a tram before too many of the beasts were on us, we'd at least have a chance.

"Agnes says that we should use the portal," Reaper yelled back, hot on my heels.

"It's only for emergencies, Reap," I reminded him as we hit the steps that led down to the subway. Then I muttered, "Stupid turtle."

"Yes, Agnes," he called out, "I agree that this does feel like an emergency."

Damn it, the turtle was right.

Wasn't it bad enough that I had a reaper for a partner? Now I had a reaper *and* a turtle? And the fact that the turtle appeared to be the smarter of the two didn't help. Shit, she was possibly the smartest of all three of us.

Bitch.

Great. Now I was referring to a turtle as a bitch.

"Fine," I said as we hit the bottom landing. "Let's portal out."

We were only seconds away from being overrun by an angry mob of rioters, before the world faded away.

CHAPTER 7

*A*fter notifying the chief that another riot had broken out, Reaper and I headed down to talk to our lead technician. We needed answers and Pecker was the only one likely to help us find them.

Pecker was a goblin who had a large office on the lowest level of the PPD building. The place was incessantly a mess. Papers were everywhere, machines or parts of machines littered the floors and desks, and there was a smell to the place that only a mother could love. He had a narrow face that was gray and covered with creases and wrinkles. His ears were pointy and long with hair growing out of them, and his nose was wide and flat, hanging down with a hook over his puffy lips.

In a nutshell, he was what you'd expect a goblin to look like.

"Ah, Piper," he said with a mischievous wink, "I just finished thinking about you roughly ten minutes ago."

"Ew," I replied, knowing full well what he meant. "That's gross."

"How can love ever be gross?" he asked, batting his eyelash. Yes, I meant that as singular. Pecker didn't have eyelashes, per se. Rather, he just had one long hair poking out from his left eye. "You are ever mysterious, my sweet."

I leaned in menacingly. "How would you like me to attach your balls to a car battery and turn on the ignition?"

"Sounds delightful," he swooned. "I'll bring the wine."

Damn it. I should have known better than to try those types of threats on him. He was an odd one. To be fair, though, I couldn't help but feel that I'd miss it if he ever quit trying to get into my pants. No, I wouldn't ever actually let him bone me...in fact, that thought alone was enough to make me want to throw up, but at least it felt nice that his feelings toward me were genuine.

It was just a shame that there was no attraction from my side of the fence.

"Anyway," I said, removing my glare, "we have an issue and we need your help."

"Anything for my favorite Retrievers," Pecker replied. "What can I do for you?"

"There are riots going on in the main city center," Reaper answered and then looked at Pecker. "I'm sure you already know about this, but we saw something interesting that we believe caused a new riot to begin."

Pecker nodded. "And?"

"There was a fae wearing a hat," Reaper finished, as if that explained everything.

"Right," Pecker stated. "Well, that's not a lot to go on. Got anything more?"

"What he's trying to say," I interjected, "is that fae don't typically hide themselves. Plus, this particular fae dropped a device that sent out a massive energy wave. Almost immediately after she did that, the people went mental."

"I see," Pecker said, tapping on the tip of his nose. It dripped onto his lab coat with each touch. "Where was this?"

We gave him the coordinates and he moved over to his computer. His fingers flew across the keyboard so fast that they were a blur. Those were some fingers that could make a lady…

Ew.

I shuddered.

Within seconds, there were video feeds pulling up from all over the area, each in their own little window.

"How long ago?" he asked out of the corner of his mouth.

"Twenty minutes or so," I answered.

The feeds were rewinding super fast. We watched as people attacked each other in reverse all the way until the peaceful moment before the storm.

Pecker paused the feed and started jumping from camera to camera.

"There she is," I said, touching the screen.

He gently removed my finger and then wiped the fingerprint away with a cloth.

Once he was done with that, he zoomed in and went frame by frame as the fae lowered to the ground. Sure enough, right in front of her was a small disc. She pressed on the top of it and a thin green light began to spin.

"Agnes says she senses something is wrong again," Reaper stated, jolting both Pecker and me from our study of the screen. "No, wait, she said that it doesn't seem real this time."

"That's because we're just watching it on the screen, Reap," I noted.

"Ah, yes."

So the turtle wasn't all that brilliant, after all, though she *did* backtrack and say that it didn't seem to be real. It wasn't like she could see the screen from within Reaper's pocket.

I rolled my eyes.

"Who's Agnes?" Pecker asked.

I found this question odd being that Reaper considered Pecker to be one of his better friends. You would think Pecker would have been the first to know about Reaper's beloved pet. Then again, there was something I'd read in goblin lore during my Retriever training that said goblins didn't get along with reptiles. Chances were that Reaper had known this, too, as he suddenly looked concerned.

"She's just an informant, of sorts," I stated, realizing that I was protecting a fucking turtle. "Nobody you'd know."

He snorted. "And she speaks to you in real-time while not even in the room?"

"Uh..."

Pecker spun around, giving us a serious look. "You guys on funny-weed or something?" he asked. "And, if so, you got any extra?"

I turned and looked at Reaper, giving him a dull stare. He opened his mouth a couple of times and finally his shoulders sagged.

With a bit of effort, my partner opened his coat, reached into his pocket, and gingerly pulled forth Agnes.

"Oh, cool," Pecker said with wide eyes. "That's a turtle, right?"

Both Reaper and I were confused by this reaction. Maybe goblins *didn't* despise reptiles?

"Yes, she's a red—"

"Red-eared slider," Pecker finished for him. "I know. I did a bunch of reading up on these things when I was trying to get into the force." He was studying Agnes while smiling. "Goblins aren't known for getting along with reptiles, you know."

"So we've heard," I said, shrugging at Reaper. "You don't seem to mind, though."

"Not at all," he trilled. "I think they're awesome, especially the ones who talk to you."

Okay, so that *seriously* caught our attention. Even Agnes twisted her head and gave Pecker the once-over.

"Wait," Pecker chuckled while pointing at Agnes, "is she a talker?"

Reaper nodded. So did I. So did Agnes.

"Oh, that's fucking cool as shit." Pecker clapped his hands together. "You're one lucky dude, Reap. Not very many talking turtles out in the world."

"I didn't know that," Reaper replied. "I thought they were all talkers."

"Nah, man." Pecker dropped back into his chair and opened a new browser window. "You see, there are—"

"Stop!" I commanded. "This isn't the time to discuss talking turtles. We have riots going on out there, remember?"

"Right," said Pecker with a twinge. "Sorry."

We got back to the task at hand, studying all of the different areas where riots had broken out. It took about an hour before we had everything we needed to present our evidence to the chief. We would have been done so sooner, but Pecker was holding Agnes with one hand while typing with the other. He still typed faster than most do with both hands, but it slowed our search down a bit.

"Listen," Pecker said as we were about to leave, "it's probably not safe for Agnes to go out with you on missions and such. If you want me to watch her while you're gone, I'd be happy to do it." He held her up. "She's fantastic."

"Are you sure?" Reaper asked, not looking excited about the idea. "I wouldn't want to impose."

"I'd love to!" Pecker then held up Agnes and looked in her eyes. "Assuming she's okay with it, of course."

Agnes nodded.

"That's settled, then," Pecker said, all smiles. "Don't worry. I'll make sure she doesn't get into any mischief."

Reaper and I walked into the elevator, leaving our lead tech along with the wonder turtle to their work.

"Isn't Pecker just the greatest?" said Reaper with a look of elation.

I sniffed. "Honestly, Reap. You need to learn to choose your words a little more carefully."

CHAPTER 8

Chief Carter didn't look much better than he had earlier in the day. There were multiple pink bottles on his desk now, and all of them appeared to be empty. I couldn't imagine drinking that much of the stuff was healthy, but the chief didn't seem to care.

"I sent a small squad down to the Diamond District, thanks to your report," he said tiredly. "What else have you got for me?"

"We think we know who is causing all of these riots, Chief," I answered and then tilted my head to the side. "Well, not *precisely* who, but we're pretty sure it stems from the fae faction."

He seemed taken aback by that. "Seriously?"

"Yeah, why?" I asked with a frown.

"Just that in all my years on the PPD, I've never had to deal with a major fae issue." He sat back and crossed his arms over his ample stomach. "They're usually so self-involved that they don't play around in faction politics." He grunted. "They'll still kick your butt if you go into their area, of course, but they're not known for branching out."

There was no arguing that.

I didn't really have any fae as friends, so it wasn't like I was able to keep a pulse on the things they were doing under the blankets, as it were. Actually, I didn't really have any friends at all. I guess Reaper was as close to a friend as I could imagine. Most people were either co-workers or acquaintances.

Anyway, my point was that I didn't hang around a lot of fae.

But it was my job to know the idiosyncrasies of each faction on a general level. This wasn't that complicated seeing that they were all pretty unique in their makeup.

Pixies were generally assholes who cursed like sailors, vampires were generally assholes who believed they were better than everyone else, werewolves were generally assholes who believe they had the right to feed on whomever they wished, djinn were...

Okay, okay, so let's just go with the point that *all* the factions were generally assholes.

Fae, though, had the distinction of keeping away from others. Stereotypically, anyway. They were similar to vampires in their belief that they were better than everyone else, but where the vampires leveraged this self-important vision to try and rule over other factions, fae pulled away from the rest of the world so as not to be tainted by them.

But that didn't mean there wasn't something nefarious going on under the covers, and that's why it would have been helpful to have friends, or at least contacts, in the

Netherworld who may have a pulse on such things. This was one of the many reasons that a beat cop down here had the advantage over a full-fledged Retriever. They kept up on things; we didn't.

"So what makes you think the fae are involved?" the chief asked.

Reaper got there first. "Remember that when we reported the fresh riot in the Diamond District, we also told you we saw that fae detonate the charge?"

"Yeah, but that's just one of them," the chief replied. "While it's still odd for a fae to get involved in things, it doesn't mean their entire faction is in on it."

"Agreed," I said with a nod, "which is why we went to do a little research with Pecker. It turns out that every one of the riots had a fae on the scene, and each of them had placed one of those energy pulses on the ground and activated it."

The chief chewed his lip as his brow creased seriously. He was obviously bouncing around ideas, utilizing his years of experience in the process.

"Was it the same fae?" he asked finally.

"No," answered Reaper. "Unless they are extremely good at disguises."

"The one in the Diamond District *was* wearing a baseball cap," I pointed out.

"True," Reaper agreed, "but that's not much of a costume."

It was for a fae.

Still, Reaper was right.

In order to look like all of the different fae we'd seen on video, it would require an amazing amount of makeup

JOHN P. LOGSDON & CHRISTOPHER P. YOUNG

and adjustments. A wizard or mage could do it, but I found it really difficult to believe that a fae would subject themselves to such physical tinkering. Just the wearing of a hat was probably painful enough.

"They were all different, Chief," I stated as fact. "Taller, shorter, thin, thinner..." There weren't any overweight fae that I was aware of, only varied levels of thin. "Different genders, too. And not all of them wore baseball caps."

"Some wore Stetsons and others top hats," noted Reaper. "It made me consider purchasing a top hat of my own, actually."

The chief and I gave him a funny look. To be fair, a top hat would probably suit Reaper quite well.

The chief grunted. "I don't get it. What's with the hats?"

"I just think it would make me look—"

"Not *your* purchasing of a hat, Officer Payne," the chief interrupted. "I'm asking why the fae would be wearing the damn things?"

It wasn't common for the chief to use strong language. And, yes, a word like "damn" was somewhat advanced for him.

"Honestly, hadn't considered it," I answered. "But if your officers can lay their hands on any of them, they should definitely try and figure it out. If there's more to it than mere disguises, it'd be good to know that."

I pushed over the images of each fae that we'd been able to get a decent photo of from the feeds. They weren't crisp, but they were better than a composite sketch. If the chief could get those photos out, maybe the cops could spot one of them.

"We think that—" I started.

The chief held up a finger. "Incoming call."

He cleared his throat and looked up, obviously listening through his connector. After a minute or so of "mmm-hmmm" and "right, right," Chief Carter pinched the bridge of his nose and let out a long breath. Finally, he said, "Okay, thanks for the report. I'll get someone on it."

"What's up, Chief?" I asked, having the feeling that something dire had happened.

He glanced up at me and then over at Reaper.

"Brazen and Kix are missing."

CHAPTER 9

*A*nyone who knows me will tell you that I'm not the biggest fan of either Brazen or Kix, but they were on my team now and that meant I had to care about their well being. Besides, they'd proven themselves to be worthy cops over the last couple of months. I'd even have to go as far as to say they were assets. There were many other names that weren't quite as positive, too, but that was a given.

"Where were they?" I asked while trying to keep my cool.

"The fae district," the chief replied. "That's where they were last seen, anyway. It was their assignment, and based on your recent intel it's the only place that makes sense."

"Fuck," I said and then covered my mouth as the chief glared at me. "Sorry."

"We must go after them," Reaper announced, standing up and heading for the door. He looked back at me. "Are you coming?"

"I'm not even breathing heavy," I replied in knee-jerk fashion. I then grunted. "Sorry. Bad joke."

Reaper frowned. "I don't get it."

My gut reaction was the same as Reaper's. We should immediately get out there and bring in the members of our team. But the chief had been pretty clear about the fact that there were only a handful of experienced Retrievers left. If we got captured too, that would cut down the numbers even further.

Plus...

"You're not allowed in the faction areas, Officer Payne," the chief stated.

That.

"We're not?"

"We're not," I answered for the chief. "We don't have the needed training and qualifications, Reap. And even if we did, you're a reaper and I'm a human. Yes, we have badges that mark us as cops, but the factions have disallowed us to enter their particular areas."

"Racism, then?"

"Down here it's just a way of life, Reap," I reminded him. "Officer Dex was the last one allowed into one of the race-specific areas back during his training days, but that was long ago and what happened with him kind of sullied it for you and me."

He creased his lips. "Then send in other Retrievers."

I'd never seen Reaper speak so firmly to the chief before. It was like he'd grown a set of balls or something. I didn't even know he'd had balls until Mrs. Donaldson tried to kick them through the top of his head. And now he appeared to be using them, metaphorically speaking. Maybe the old woman had activated them somehow? Honestly, I had no idea how men even carried those damn things around.

"There are already other officers on the way to check on them," the chief said in a gentle tone. "We'll get information from them soon enough."

Reaper was clearly not pleased with this answer. I had never known how much team loyalty meant to him. It wasn't like I didn't feel the same way, but there were rules that...

I sat up suddenly.

What the fuck had happened to me?

Rules?

Since when did I give a shit about rules?

That was my team out there. Yeah, they were a couple of dicks, but they were my team. *I* should have been the one fuming at the moment, not Reaper.

"Chief," I said, getting to my feet, "Reap's right."

"I am?"

"Brazen and Kix are part of my squad."

"*Our* squad," Reaper mumbled.

"Huh?" I gave him a sidelong glance. "Oh, right. Yeah. *Our* squad."

A little flash of something crossed Chief Carter's face. It was fleeting and barely noticeable, but if I were to make a guess as to what it was, I'd have to say...pride?

"You're both forbidden to go to the fae area," he said aloud while writing something on a piece of paper. "You have no jurisdiction in the Netherworld."

He turned the paper toward us.

I can't protect either of you. If you're captured, the fae will be well within their rights to kill you.

"The rules are very strict on this subject," he continued his verbal rant while writing on another page. "You don't have the necessary training to enter race-specific areas."

Stay in the shadows as much as possible and you may have a chance. I can't afford to lose either of you.

"Now, I don't want to hear another word about this," he said after we'd finished reading his note. "Am I clear?"

"Yes, sir," Reaper and I replied in unison.

"Good."

He then scribbled out something else.

Good luck.

CHAPTER 10

*W*e took the tubes to the city center nearest the fae faction, being careful to converse via an encrypted direct connection.

Speaking aloud would only draw the attention from others on the tram, and I was always leery to use a non-encrypted channel when something was this important. While nobody was *supposed* to listen in or record any private conversations that were held via the connectors, I would bet that people did. Call me a conspiracy theorist if you want, but I believed the powers-that-be did whatever they wanted, whenever they wanted, and however they wanted…using the justification that their actions were for the greater good.

Riiight.

Each race-specific area was essentially a small city connected to the larger central city. Some had gates and walls, others used fencing, the mages used spells, and some were left wide open, almost inviting trouble.

Faeland, as I liked to call it, went with walls and a gated entrance.

"What's the plan?" asked Reaper, bringing my mind back to the present.

I gave him a concerned look. *"Uh...sneak into the area, find Brazen and Kix, and get them out of there."*

"I know that, Piper," he replied with a look. *"But isn't there something specific?"*

"There really isn't."

I'd learned long ago that planning left you blocked for improvisation, especially when you were dealing with noobs on the force. Reaper was good, yes, but he was still green. To be fair, down here I was pretty green myself. I knew topside like the back of my hand, including how to deal with the people who lived there. But this was a completely different ball of wax.

We weren't supposed to be going into race-specific areas down here. The chief was clear about that. It was in the Netherworld rules. Retrievers were topside; there were PPD precincts topside to deal with supers living there, but Netherworld cops dealt with Netherworld issues. While the standard Netherworld police *was* allowed topside under special circumstances, such as training or if they would be instrumental in catching a particular criminal, the same courtesy was not easily leant to Retrievers. It *did* happen from time to time, but it took a fair bit of paperwork and approvals. These rules were in place because Netherworld officers had to go through faction retraining and qualifiers every six months. They had to pass tests and everything. All cops who passed these tests were granted access as long as they either followed the rules or had a warrant *and* followed the rules. As the chief had noted, Retrievers didn't have this training requirement and so we weren't allowed in.

"*Piper,*" Reaper said in a monotone voice as the tram began to slow, "*I would truly feel much better if we had a plan.*"

I rolled my eyes at him and groaned.

"*What would a plan buy us, Reap?*" I asked incredulously. "*We'll create it, start enacting it, and then find out that we've managed to get hemmed in by it. I don't know about you, but I don't think that keeping to a plan if we get stuck in a corner is going to work.*"

"*I see your point,*" he said after a moment, "*but going by the seat of our pants—I hope I'm using that in the proper context—may result in our being unprepared for whatever may come.*"

"*By the very fact that your statement denotes we have no idea what may come, how would you suggest we plan for it?*" I countered and then nodded at him. "*And you used that phrase properly, by the way.*"

The tram stopped and the doors opened.

People began pouring out into the underground level of the subway as others waited to get inside.

The place was rather nondescript. It had beige tiled walls with matching floors. Aside from the Diamond District, it was one of the cleaner stops I'd seen. There were two escalators on either side of the large space, both with up and down options. There were also stairs running alongside the escalators, and an elevator sat near the back in the center of the space.

Bodies were pulsing through the underbelly of the city

like blood through veins. Faces were staring at smart phones and tablets for the most part, but those who weren't tethered to their electronic leashes kept their gazes straight forward. Now and then a vampire would give us a haughty look, but that was to be expected.

"*I assumed we'd see more fae here,*" Reaper said.

"*Just because we're nearest the fae area, we're still in the city center,*" I replied. "*The actual fae faction is about a mile from here.*"

"*Right,*" he said, looking frustrated. "*I actually knew that, but...*" He trailed off.

Reaper had spent the majority of his career in the Netherworld working in the records room of the Paranormal Police Department. He'd never been a beat cop, having bypassed that training due to his special skills, life experience, and ability to use an advanced tattoo system that Pecker had set up for him. So he had no real street knowledge of the area, and he'd obviously been smart enough to know better than to leave the city center in all his years down here.

"*It's okay, Reap,*" I said, feeling like I needed to say something. "*I'm edgy, too. Just remember that we're both immortal and that we both have skills that the fae don't know about.*"

"*I suppose so.*"

"*I know so,*" I avowed. "*We'll be just fine...I hope.*"

We got to the top of the escalator and moved outside.

There *were* more fae in this area than other races, but that was only because of how close we were to their race-specific area.

"*Notice anything odd, Reap?*" I asked while scanning around.

"*No rioting.*"

"*Exactly.*"

"*What do you think that means?*" he asked.

"*You tell me, Reap,*" I answered. "*Why would this area not be seeing the same level of turbulence as the others?*"

"*Because our assessment of the situation was correct. The fae are responsible for what's going on down here.*"

"*Yep.*"

"*Then again,*" he added, "*we don't know if any of the other areas have been as unaffected as this one.*"

"*That's true,*" I agreed, "*but something tells me any of those places not already dealing with riots right now will be soon.*"

After one last look around, I strode purposefully toward Faeland.

CHAPTER 11

e could see the guards at the gate, but they couldn't see us. That's because we picked a spot behind a tall hedge and were peeking around it.

"I'm assuming you're not planning to walk up and ask if Brazen and Kix are in there," Reaper whispered. Then he looked at me with a concerned expression. "You're not going to do that, right?"

I squinted at him. "No."

There had to be another way in besides the front gate. I'd often heard that the different factions had secret entrances—or exits, depending on your perspective. Apparently this had to do with needing a way in or out in the event of a large-scale attack. No doubt those access points, if they existed, would be protected by runes, but I'd be able to see those. I couldn't bypass them, other than via brute force, but spotting them was half the problem.

"*Pecker,*" I said through the connector as an idea struck, "*I don't suppose you know of any fae who are PPD-friendly?*"

"*I know a couple who* say *they are, Piper,*" he replied, "*but it's difficult to tell. Why, what's up?*"

"*We need to get into Faeland, but we don't want to go through the front gate.*"

"*Ah,*" he said and then there was a pause. "*I doubt you'll find any fae to help with that, but...*" Another pause. Clearly he was working on something. "*There are a ton of records in the databases here regarding various tidbits of information for each faction.*"

"*Including entryways?*" asked Reaper.

"*It includes everything,*" answered Pecker, "*assuming it's been entered into the system, of course. That's going to be the trick. Give me a sec.*"

As Pecker started digging around for information on Faeland, I dragged Reaper away from our position overlooking the main gate and started walking the perimeter.

The high wall stayed to our right, and I made sure to keep far enough away from it so as not to draw the ire of any fae, while staying close enough to give me the ability to seek out runes. We'd barely made it one hundred steps before I saw a distortion by the wall.

It was a hidden zone. I couldn't see past those zones, but I was able to detect their presence. Again, this was one of those special skills that I'd shared with my now deceased parents. I didn't know what it was about our particular genetic makeup, but being a normal who could see supers, spot runes, and detect null and hidden zones had made us targets on Keller's hit list many years ago. My parents didn't survive. I did, but only because of my immortality...at least that was my guess.

So I couldn't say what was behind that zone, but I knew it was there. If I had to make a guess, I'd bet on an entryway, likely covered with detection runes.

My first thought was to boldly step through and see what was on the other side. But a quick glance up told me there were cameras all over the place. Whether or not anyone was manning them, I couldn't say, but they did seem to be following me and Reaper as we continued our stroll.

"Could we not request the aid of a wizard on the force?" asked Reaper aloud. "I've heard a few names discussed over my years on the force. Elsa Jones, Willis Argent, and Timothy Methkins are usually available for freelance work."

Only because they were all nearly impossible to manage. The solid wizards got snapped up quickly, leaving these three to those who either had lower-profile cases or who were still bottom feeders on the force.

Jones hated working with other women, or maybe it was just me. The last time we got paired up, we nearly killed each other. Well, technically, I nearly killed her, but she got in a few decent scratches before it was all said and done.

Argent was renowned for his ability to create amazing fireworks shows, but he was essentially pointless in police work. Great for distractions, though.

Methkins also had a reputation that put him on the only-if-I-have-no-other-options list. He was nice enough, but where most wizards were scatterbrained, this guy was on an entirely different level. It was so bad, in fact, that most cops just called him "Meth."

I *knew* the guy, but he was the only one of the three that I'd not yet worked beside, so I couldn't say how he'd perform professionally. On reputation alone, I'd probably kill him before the day was through.

Still, I'd rather risk him than another bout with Elsa, and Argent would be so flamboyant that we'd be spotted almost instantly.

"*I got nothing here, Piper,*" Pecker announced after a few minutes. "*There are a few places mentioned for vampires, werewolves, and djinn, but nothing on the fae. They're pretty close-lipped, though.*"

"*All right,*" I said with a sigh. "*Thanks for checking.*"

"*No problem, baby,*" he purred, causing me to gag. "*Oh, by the way, Reap,*" Pecker said, changing topics, "*Agnes is doing great. She helped me figure out one of the algorithms I've been struggling with for the last few months.*"

"*That's nice to hear,*" Reaper said, looking proud. "*I am ever in awe regarding her abilities. There are many things she's capable of, but nobody would ever know it since they just see her as nothing but a turtle.*" He chuckled lightly. "*She is rather clever, though.*"

"*I'll say. Listen, you can feel free to bring her into the office every day, if you want. I could certainly use the help.*"

Reaper was beaming now.

"*I'll talk to the chief about it,*" he said. "*Thanks for watching her, Pecker.*"

"*Not a problem. Later.*"

I wanted to broach the subject of how silly it was that a turtle was capable of solving math puzzles, but seeing that she was telepathic, too, I really didn't have much to stand on. Maybe I was just jealous because I'd never had a pet that did more than eat, shit, and sleep. Add "have sex" to that list and it'd describe nearly every boyfriend I'd had prior to going with my one-night-stands-only rule.

"Do me a favor and see if you can get Meth down here, Reap," I said. "I'm going to keep focused on spotting zones."

"Meth?"

"Methkins," I clarified.

"Ah."

CHAPTER 12

*M*ethkins arrived twenty minutes later, just after I'd completed finding all the sections I suspected would allow us sneaky access into Faeland.

The guy was short by wizard standards, coming in around shoulder height to me. His face was covered in a slurry of pockmarks that showed the history of his adolescent battle with acne. There was no beard or mustache, but he did appear to be in need of a shave. He had a unibrow that sat over the most brilliant green eyes I'd ever seen. Instead of wearing a robe and pointed hat like a lot of wizards, Methkins had on jeans and an Iron Maiden T-shirt, and he was so thin that I imagined he'd have to run around in the shower just to get wet.

It was all of this, and his inability to stay focused on anything for more than ten seconds, that garnered him the nickname "Meth."

"Hey, guys," he said in a stoner sort of way. "How's it hangin'?"

"How is what hanging?" asked Reaper while looking over his own body.

"Everything is fine," I said before Meth could answer the question. It'd just start a discussion that we didn't have time for at the moment. "I've spotted a number of potential access points down here," I added, pointing at the wall, "but I need someone who can disable runes as needed." I gave Methkins a tight look. "Can you do that for us?"

"Sure, man," he said, nodding as he scanned the area. "They got them hotdog trucks on this side? I gotta get my food on."

I blinked at him and crossed my arms.

"Uh-oh," he said, giving me the once-over. "You pissed or something?"

"I didn't bring you down here to eat hotdogs, Meth," I asserted, wondering if he could even get a hotdog down anyway. "We have a couple of officers who have been captured. Each minute that goes by is a minute that they could be getting tortured...or worse."

"Worse?" he said with his eyebrows up. "You mean like they might be making them wait to eat or somethin'?"

I went to take a step toward the little twerp, but Reaper must have realized I was getting wound up. He stepped in the way and pulled Methkins aside.

"You are hungry, yes?" Reaper asked.

"Yeah, dude. I got the grumbles somethin' fierce."

Reaper paused for a moment, obviously trying to process what Methkins meant by that. Eventually, he just shrugged and squared his shoulders.

"I will gladly give you the money for a couple of hotdogs, if you will first disable some runes for us."

"You need me to disable runes?"

"Oh, for the love of…" I started, reaching out for the little shit.

He ducked away and moved to stand behind Reaper.

"What's her beef?"

"My beef, you fuck twit," I spat, "is that we need to get in there to save a couple of lives and you're more worried about eating than you are with helping us!"

"Oh, right." He wiped his nose. "So what do you want me to do?"

I bit my lip and fought to keep myself from shoving Reaper out of the way so I could strangle the scrawny twerp.

It wouldn't help.

While we *were* in a rush, it was clear that Methkins didn't share the same sense of urgency. Me threatening to remove his head from his body wouldn't help. Well, it may help *me*, but it wouldn't get the job done.

So I took a deep breath and slowly counted back from ten.

That's when an idea struck. Wizards were mostly laid back, but whenever you went and started comparing them to each other, they got ultra competitive.

"You know," I said, glancing away, "I remember when I was new to the force there was a wizard who was the fastest at breaking down runes." I tapped on my chin in pretend thought. "He was the best. I think his name was Kimo, but I'm not sure if that was it or not."

"Yep," Methkins said. "Kimo kills it at opening these

things. Also makes a mean stew. The dude rocks." He snapped his fingers. "Maybe you shoulda called him down here to help you guys out?"

Clearly catching on to the circumstance at hand, Reaper took a step back and motioned for me to go ahead and kick Methkins' ass.

When Methkins noticed his protector had moved away, he changed his tune.

"Uh...so where are these runes?" he asked as his eyes shifted back and forth between Reaper and me. "I can always do some foodin' later."

Without a word, I pointed to the nearest hidden zone.

He began to walk toward it, but I grabbed his shoulder and turned to stroll parallel to the wall.

"What are you doin', man?"

"There are cameras on the posts near the top," I explained. "If the fae spot us, it won't be an advantage to have broken through the runes."

"Oh, yeah. That makes sense." He scratched his greasy hair. "What do you want to do, then?"

"I was hoping that you may have some ideas on the subject," I replied, though I had serious doubts that he'd come up with anything useful. "You *are* a wizard, after all."

"True." He rubbed his chin as we continued our slow pace. A smile formed within seconds and he glanced up at me. "We could get some hotdogs."

It took some effort, but Reaper finally pulled me away from Methkins. I hadn't done any real damage to the wizard, but I had the feeling he wasn't going to mention hotdogs again any time soon.

Unfortunately, the look on his face said that he had no desire to help me out at this point either.

"What the fuck, man?" he said as he brushed at his shirt. "Why are you being a dick?"

"Friend," Reaper interjected, trying again, "I am a person whom you will find to be very patient, but you can see that my partner is not like I am."

"You can say that again, dude. She's in serious need of a chill pill."

Reaper turned to me and direct-connected.

"*I don't believe this is going to work,*" he said.

"*You sure?*" I said with much sarcasm.

"*I am...*" He paused and glanced up. "*Wait, that was sarcasm, yes?*"

I nodded.

"*Ah, well, even if we get Methkins to do his job, he is going to be difficult through the entire journey.*"

That was difficult to argue.

"*Fine. What do you suggest we do?*"

He grinned. "*I have a plan for that.*"

"*Yikes.*"

CHAPTER 13

*W*e stood back near the main entrance and I wasn't feeling the warm and fuzzies.

"You sure this is going to work?" I asked in a whisper.

Methkins was seated on a bench behind us, just out of earshot. We'd explained to him that there was a food truck nearby, but we had to do something first. It seemed to sate his cravings to learn he was going to get food.

Fucking wizards.

"It's the only place we can portal in where their systems won't detect the transference," Reaper replied, "and it's clear that we're not going to be able to utilize Mr. Methkins as we had originally intended."

"True," I agreed.

The fact was that time was running short. Honestly, it was probably too late already, but we had to at least try. I was still baffled by the fact that I was putting my ass on the line for Brazen anyway. Kix was one thing, but Brazen? Ugh.

"Fine," I said finally. "This is your plan, so I'll step back and let you do your thing."

He gave me a worried look. That, in turn, made me worried.

"What is it, Reap?"

"I'm not very adept at falsehoods, Piper," he explained.

"So you want me to lie to him?"

He shrugged. "You're okay with that sort of thing."

I shook my head at my partner. It was kind of a dickish move to have me do his dirty work. Technically, I had no qualms lying to Methkins if it meant getting us into Faeland, but for Reaper to just assume I was cool with lying was a bit douchey.

"You *do* realize that asking me to lie on your behalf makes me nothing more than a proxy for you, right?"

"I do," he replied without inflection, "and I'm okay with that."

Obviously, reapers rationalized their behavior differently than the rest of us.

"Fine," I said, "let's do this."

Reaper and I headed over to where Methkins was seated, which was a half block down and across the main walkway. It was far enough away from the main gates, but they were still visible from here.

The little wizard kept a wary eye on me, which made sense considering I wanted to kick him into tomorrow. But I had to play it cool.

"Look," I said, hating every second of playing the game, "I'm sorry I got hotheaded back there. It's just that I've got a couple of cops inside that place who are probably in the process of dying."

"Yeah, that's what you said before," Methkins replied with a slow nod. His stomach grumbled loudly. "Still, I need some chow, dig?"

Suddenly, lying to the creep didn't bug me so much.

"About that," I said after a quick glance at Reaper, "the guards at that gate over there know where you can find that food truck."

Methkins looked around me at the gates.

"Those guys know?"

"Yep," I said. "We just heard them talking about wanting to...uh...get their food on, too."

"No foolin'?"

"Ask Reaper," I said, flicking my thumb at my partner. "He heard them, too. Didn't ya, Reap?"

Reaper jolted a bit, but I couldn't help myself. He had to get his hands at least a little dirty in this play of his.

"Well," he began, "it *is* about time for most people to eat, right?"

I raised an appraising eyebrow at him. He'd skirted the edge nicely.

"Is for me," groaned Methkins.

"Exactly," I said encouragingly, helping him to his feet. He winced at first but then realized I wasn't going to hit him again. "So if you go over there and talk to those fine guards, I'm sure that you can get your order in with them for a nice round of hotdogs."

"Sweet," he said, heading off toward the guards.

We crossed the road and then slid back up to our place behind the hedge.

"Do you think they'll hurt him?" asked Reaper.

"Only if we're lucky," I replied, but then caught that

Reaper was uneasy. It was *his* plan, after all. "Don't worry, Reap. They'll just give him an earful for being so close to their area, and then they'll shoo him away. After that, Meth'll come looking for us, but we'll already be inside by then."

"You're sure?"

"Of course I'm sure," I said.

I wasn't sure.

The gate opened and a few guards poured out, moving to flank Methkins. Fortunately, he was smart enough to stay behind the red line that said, "Only fae allowed beyond this point." This meant that the guards couldn't legally touch the wizard. Whether or not they'd honor that rule was anyone's guess, though, and considering the fact that they were clearly responsible for the riots going on in the city at the moment, I was doubtful that they'd adhere to basic law.

But that wasn't my worry at the moment.

"We're clear, Reap," I announced. Once those gates opened, the field around that area of the blockade dropped. That meant we could safely portal in without being detected. "Get us in there."

"Huh?" he replied and then shook himself back to the mission. "Oh, right. Sorry. I was just..." He stopped and cleared his throat.

It took him a couple of seconds to get the portal set.

I put my arm on his shoulder and he hit the final button.

The world faded and reappeared.

We were standing near some bushes inside Faeland

now. A quick glance around told us that we were in the clear.

The gates were still visible from here, but we were now seeing the backs of the guards. We still needed to be really careful here, though. There were likely cameras around and probably sentries as well.

"Okay," I said, "we have to keep near the path and do our best not to be seen."

"Right," Reaper agreed, motioning me forward.

"Hey, man," I heard Methkins yelling, "let go of me!"

We spun back and saw the fae guards were dragging him through the gates.

He must have crossed that line.

"Shit," I hissed, knowing full well that Reaper was going to feel responsible for that idiot's capture.

As if we didn't have enough problems already.

CHAPTER 14

*R*eaper and I waited for the guards to pass by, dragging a cuffed Methkins with them, before we started to move.

"I can't help but feel responsible for his capture," Reaper said in a forlorn tone of voice. *"We'll have to do what we can to get him free."*

My initial reaction regarding saving Methkins was "Fuck that guy," but his getting snagged was actually a good thing for us.

Hopefully, anyway.

"Let's keep on those guards," I said, carefully avoiding any commitment to saving Methkins. If it came down to choosing between him and my two officers, there'd be no contest. *"I'm hoping they're going to take him to the same place they have Brazen and Kix."*

"Yes," agreed Reaper. *"That makes sense."*

The trek wasn't a long one, but we were only able to follow so far before the trees ended and the city began.

I'd seen pictures online of the fae city many times over my life. They paled in comparison to the real thing.

This place was stunning.

The buildings were coated with textures and paintings that tickled the eye. Colored windows complemented each structure perfectly. Where most architects in both the Netherworld and Overworld went with the standard blocky building look, these had panache. There were deeply rounded edges, curves, spirals, and combinations of all three. It was clear that the most stunning people in the Netherworld also had an eye for architectural brilliance.

And the city was clean.

There wasn't a dirty-looking piece of ground within eyesight.

"They've taken him into the one that's shaped like a 'C,'" Reaper said, pointing to the second building on the right.

"Good," I said, ripping my eyes away from the intense beauty and refocusing on the task at hand. *"We'll go around the back and slip inside."*

We moved slowly, keeping an eye out for sentries and cameras. Guards were easy to spot and even easier to circumvent, but cameras weren't all that simple. I also kept my eyes open for runes. There weren't likely to be any around, but I didn't want to chance it. Most factions in the Netherworld were exceptionally paranoid, after all. They had good reason to be.

Once we'd cleared the edge of the closest building, we found a few fae walking around.

"Those aren't guards," Reaper noted.

"No," I agreed, *"but we still need to watch our step."*

"*Yes.*"

It took us forever to slip from position to position because we had to wait for people to leave the area before making each move. Fifteen minutes later, we were in the alley beside the building that Methkins had been dragged into.

Just as we were about to risk heading inside, though, the back door opened and the two guards who had brought Methkins in were bringing him out this way.

Reaper and I kept our position in the alley and watched as they walked straight out into the field.

Methkins had clearly been roughed up during whatever they'd done to him in that building. He was bloodied and his feet were dragging with each step.

"*We have to save him, Piper,*" Reaper insisted.

"*Yeah, I know.*"

I never should have asked Reaper to bring that guy down to help us. Clearly, that had been a huge mistake on my part. Plus, Reaper was already feeling guilty over the fact that Methkins had been captured. And now that we'd both seen what the fae had done to the wizard, *and* noting that they were dragging him off somewhere that would surely end in the little twit's demise, we were officially on the hook to stop them.

Fuck.

"All right," I whispered without the connector, "we're going to go after him, Reap, but you're going to have to be ready to use force."

He shot me a look.

"Don't give me any shit about it," I warned, pointing at

him. "Once we break that little douche away from those guards, we're going to be in a world of hurt."

Reaper licked his lips and slowly nodded. Then he began to roll up his sleeves.

"I can stun the guards," he said. "That will render them incapable of calling for help."

"We could also just kill them," I pointed out.

"I'd prefer we didn't."

"You're no fun."

After Reaper had done a full scan of the area to make sure we didn't have any bogies to worry about, we took off after Methkins and the guards.

Just as we were closing in, they stopped.

We crouched and waited.

The guard on the left knelt down and began running his hand over a piece of rock. A flurry of yellow lights began running all over it. Then, after multiple flashes, a window appeared that showed a thick forest.

"That's a window, right?" I asked, not wanting to risk speaking out loud.

"Yes," Reaper replied. *"They are using some type of portal system. I have homed in on Mr. Methkins' personal signature and will do my best to track where they go."*

"Or...we could just follow in after them right now!"

I jumped up and started running.

But by the time we'd reached their location, the window had closed.

The guards and Methkins were gone.

ortunately, we were out of visual range from the main city, unless there were cameras around here, of course. I didn't see any, but that didn't mean they weren't there. Technology allowed for the tiniest remote viewing devices these days.

I was just glad there weren't any runes to deal with.

"Do you know where they went, Reap?" I asked as he studied the stone the guard had been messing with before the window appeared.

"I was unable to track Mr. Methkins when they went through." He took off his glasses and peered intently at the object. "With any luck, I'll be able to spot smudges that will demonstrate which numbers he selected to activate this thing."

I grunted. "Even if you do, you're not going to know which order he pressed them, Reap."

"You're right," he hissed. "Damn it."

Now, *that* was something you didn't hear every day. Reaper wasn't one to use foul language. Even Chief Carter could be made to sound like a drunken sailor around my partner. That told me that he was truly taking this pretty hard.

"You know you're not at fault for Methkins getting caught, right?" I asked, putting a hand on his shoulder. "The guy undoubtedly stepped over that red line and became fair game."

Reaper shrugged my hand away and stood up.

"He wouldn't have been near that line at all if we hadn't set him up."

The truth was that if Methkins had any sense at all, he would have told us to fuck off when we'd suggested he go near the line in the first place. If he hadn't been so worried about "getting his food on," we would have been able to slip through a hidden zone, and we'd be on the hunt for Brazen and Kix right now. Looking back at that stone, though, told me that if Methkins *hadn't* gotten captured, we would never have tracked down my two subordinates.

His misfortune was a lucky break for us, assuming we could open the damn window, anyway.

"*Pecker,*" I called through the connector, making sure Reaper was also hooked in, "*Meth got captured and they took him through a portal of some sort. It's controlled by a small obelisk with a keypad on it, though, and we don't know the combination.*"

"*Sucks to be you, then,*" he replied soberly. "*Those things are a bitch to crack.*"

I swallowed my pride and muttered, "*Even for a mastermind like you?*"

Reaper's eyes went wide at that, glowing like a semi-truck at night with its brights on.

"Put your damn glasses back on," I commanded aloud, "and shut up."

"I didn't say anything," he complained while putting his shades on.

Yes, he did. Just not verbally.

"*You think I'm a mastermind, eh?*" Pecker replied in a goblinesque Barry White voice. "*I never knew you thought of me like that, Piper.*"

"*I'm easily proved wrong, Pecker,*" I commented, hoping to challenge him. "*If you can't break through this code, then I'll have to reevaluate my thoughts on the matter.*"

"*And if I can break through, what say we have a drink to discuss my mastermindedness?*"

"*That's not even a word,*" I pointed out, trying to rattle him a little.

"*You knew what I meant, right?*"

"*Well, yes, but—*"

"*A word is a word if the person receiving it comprehends its meaning. How else do you think new words are invented?*"

He had me there. It wasn't like civilization blinked into existence with a full vocabulary that everyone understood. Hell, if that were true, there'd be no need for different languages, or everyone would understand all that was being said anyway.

"*Fine, if you can get us through the portal here by breaking into this damn thing, we'll do drinks.*" I then quickly added, "*If you can't, though, I'm going to expect you to admit you suffer from idiotedness.*"

"*You could have just said 'idiocy,' Piper,*" he remarked.

"*We're waiting,*" I said flatly.

We sent him snapshots of the device, checked ground connections, and measured distances between where the window was in relation to the obelisk. Reaper had also pointed out the smudge marks on the device in an effort to give Pecker more information.

Part of me wanted Pecker to fail, of course, seeing that I had no real desire to go out for drinks with him.

But I'd do it if that meant getting through that damn portal.

"*Okay, okay,*" he said in an excited voice. "*Agnes and I were working on it here and she's found a solution. Steam up that keypad with hot breath and immediately take a snapshot of it for us.*"

I did.

"*Now what?*"

"*Just a sec,*" Pecker replied. "*Running it through a scan system that Agnes came up with. Hopefully this...*" He paused. "*Got it!*"

"*Got what?*" I asked, losing my patience. "*Could you be a little more descriptive here?*"

"*Reaper was right about seeing the fingerprints that the guard left,*" answered Pecker as if he were describing his favorite *Star Wars* scene to a room full of fellow nerds. "*Agnes hypothesized that if we had a picture of the entire layout, her computer program could analyze the density of residue left by each print. The first one would have the most oil, the second would have less, the third—*"

"*Right, I get it,*" I interrupted. "*So do we have the combination or not?*"

"*We do,*" he replied, "*and you owe me a drink. Nothing fancy. Just a glass of wine at La Shay will do.*"

"*Actually,*" I countered, "*I owe Reaper and Agnes a glass of wine.* You, *my goblin friend, didn't solve the problem. They did.*"

"*Damn.*"

CHAPTER 16

*R*eaper entered in the code precisely as given and the window opened. We glanced at each other with wide eyes.

Who knew?

"Hello?" Pecker said, breaking our mesmerized silence. *"Did it work?"*

"It worked," Reaper replied. *"Give Agnes a hug for me, please."*

I'd heard of choking-the-chicken, tugging-the-turkey, and smacking-the-snake, but hugging-the-turtle was a new one. The phrase didn't even use alliteration. Still, something told me that people would probably start using that phrase on a Facebook group or something. You know how odd people can be.

Without further delay, we jumped through the portal, ready for anything.

There was no tingling sensation like when we used our portals, and the world didn't fade out and then back in again. If anything, it felt as though we'd just hopped over a patch of grass.

But it did *sound* different.

"Do you hear that?" I whispered.

"I don't hear anything," Reaper replied.

"Exactly."

He nodded in understanding.

This place was dead silent. There were no crickets or frogs or even rustling leaves. In fact, there wasn't even a breeze.

"We're in a dimensional box," I said.

These were little pieces of space that were held together via magic. They didn't technically exist, and the moment the magic died, so did everyone inside the box. Not a fun idea.

"Yes," Reaper agreed. "That means we can be tracked by whoever created it."

I felt my blood run cold at the thought.

"Assuming someone is bothering to look," I said, trying to calm myself down. "*I* would be constantly looking if this were my place, but I'm paranoid like that. People who build things like this are typically too arrogant to worry about them being broken into."

I started walking forward, heading toward an area that had lights all around it.

"Besides," I continued as we moved off the beaten path, just in case the guards headed back this way, "even if they do recognize two additional bodies, it wouldn't mean they'd know it was us."

"No, but they could determine that we aren't fae."

"Possibly," I said with a shrug, "but I don't think it's

likely. And it's irrelevant at this point anyway. We're here and we've got a job to do." I then flipped over to the connector. *"Can you hear me okay?"*

There was no response.

"Well, that's a problem," I rasped.

"What?"

"Connectors aren't working in here."

Reaper looked down for a moment. Then he squatted. And then really squatted, almost to the point where it looked like he was trying to determine the color of his asshole.

"What the hell are you doing?" I asked.

"I tried to reach you first," he said. "It didn't work. So then I got myself into a tighter shape, making for a boosted signal."

"That works?"

"Yes," he said. "Well, at least with the connector I'm outfitted with, which is admittedly different than yours."

"Ah."

"Well, I then attempted to reach a tower, but that failed, too. Finally, I worked my way into a very tight ball and tried to reach Pecker."

"That's what it looked like you were doing, Reap," I said, trying to contain my laughter. "You could break your neck going there, if you're not careful."

He tilted his head at me.

"I don't understand."

"Never mind. We'll just have to keep our voices low." I motioned him to follow me. "We need to get moving, and be ready with your stun stuff."

"Hopefully my other devices work," he said. "I can't track bodies, that's for certain."

That gave me pause, but I had no idea how he planned to test his other abilities out, and I really didn't want to see him attempt to pleasure himself again. Yes, I knew he wasn't actually doing that, but goddamn.

We reached the edge of the trees and found a set of small huts. They weren't fancy, which was surprising. For fae to use such a utilitarian place as this was odd.

That's when I caught sight of a man who was unmistakable. It was the same mage who I'd witnessed kill my parents those many years ago. It was that same fucking face that had entered my room and gave me a death smile before his magical energy failed to take me out.

It was the man I would give *almost* anything to kill.

"Keller," I whispered, almost breathless, as I pulled my gun up to aim it at him. "It's Keller."

Reaper grabbed my wrist and pushed it down.

"You're right," he said, "but if you miss or if he's shielded or if that's just a projection...we'll be found out and killed before you've had a chance to exact your revenge."

I hated it when he was right, and he seemed to be right *a lot*.

Keller was standing with a fae who looked familiar to me as well. She'd been on the news many times, in fact. Her name was Temperance, and she was the leader of the fae council.

Though she was likely hundreds of years old, you'd never know it from looking at her. If anything, she looked like she couldn't be more than twenty-five. Everything about her was perky: cheeks, shoulders, breasts, and ass. All of it firm and taut.

Bitch.

But what was she doing talking with Keller?

I knew the moment I asked myself that question how stupid it sounded. Obviously, she was working with him to cause unrest in the city. The real question was why would she risk collaborating with him? Special treatment was the only promise he could make, assuming that he planned to take over the Netherworld. And seeing that he was an evil piece of power-hungry shit, that was clearly the plan.

"We need to get closer to them," I said, looking around for a way through. "We have to hear what they're saying."

"How do you propose we do that?"

"I don't know, but..." I trailed off as the image of Keller faded away. So he *had* just been a projection. "So much for that."

"She's coming this way," Reaper said, pulling me back from the edge of the trees.

Temperance stopped beside another tent as a young man stepped out. He was grinning from ear to ear, and he had specks of blood on his white coat. Whatever he was up to couldn't have been pleasant.

"I hope you're not doing too much damage, Mr. Cleary," Temperance warned in that same voice that made male news reporters weak in the knees. "We may need those two as bargaining chips at some point."

"No, ma'am," Mr. Cleary replied. "They're not happy, but they're alive."

"Good." She flicked her wrist at one of the other tents. "There is a wizard in that one. I don't care about his life, so you may feel free to extract any information you can from him until he breathes his last."

Mr. Cleary looked like a man who had just won the lottery.

"Do try to keep his screams under control, Mr. Cleary," Temperance stated. "While I'm sure you rather enjoy your work, there are fae among us who do not have your iron constitution for such matters."

With that, Temperance turned away and sauntered back to the main tent. Mr. Cleary rushed into the hut he'd been occupying and then zoomed back out, carrying a box of what I assumed were instruments of torture.

"He's going to kill Mr. Methkins," Reaper said in a voice so cold that I shivered. "I cannot allow that."

"I know," I agreed, fighting to keep him as steady as he did with me when I wanted to fire a Death Nail at Keller. "But he's going to prolong it, Reap. Just killing Meth isn't going to make him happy enough. Let's get Brazen and Kix out of there, you heal them up as best you can, and then we'll go after Meth."

Reaper's glare on the tent that Mr. Cleary had just entered was deadly.

Something told me if the fae was holding pliers when we finally got in there, Reaper was going to shove them up the guy's ass.

CHAPTER 17

*B*razen and Kix looked pretty rough when we got into the hut. They were scarred and bloody, and there were multiple bruises on their faces. If I were being honest, I'd say it improved Brazen's looks somewhat.

Reaper and I set about unfastening their bindings.

They both slid from their chairs and onto the floor, groaning.

"Do what you can, Reap," I said, hoping that his particular skills would be effective in this place. "I'll look around for potions or whatever I can find."

I caught sight of his hands glowing lightly, which signaled that he wasn't powerless here. Whether he had the same level of power as he did outside of this place was anyone's guess, though.

Keller would have the answer to that, but there wasn't time to dwell on that asshole at the moment. I needed to focus on hunting for something we could use.

Potions.

Keys.

Weapons.

Whatever the hell I could get my hands on to get us through this and back out of here. The place we were in was so bad that I *wanted* to get back to Faeland. To be fair, Faeland *was* gorgeous, and if there weren't such strict rules about who was allowed to walk the area, I'd be the first person to book a spa day there.

A small desk sat near the back wall. It had a hutch on top that was filled with tiny drawers. It brought back a memory from my childhood. My father had a desk just like this. He kept screws, nails, wires, and various other gadgets and tidbits in it.

I shook myself and got back to searching.

Most of the drawers contained nothing, or little slips of paper with some type of odd writing on them. Even though I couldn't read the scribble, I realized it was magical, so I pocketed them. One of our wizards might be able to decipher what they were.

That, along with a shriek from the hut next door, made me think of Methkins.

Reaper glanced over at me.

"I know, I know," I said. "Keep working. The faster we're out of here, the faster we can get Meth."

I realized that sounded wrong, but I knew what I meant.

After stashing a good fifteen slips of paper, I finally hit pay dirt. The next few drawers contained vials, and they all had readable text on them.

Healing.

Rupture.

Blinding.

Energy.

Crippling.

It was abundantly clear that Mr. Cleary enjoyed his job. Bringing a person to the edge of death and then giving them healing and energy just so he could repeat the process was seriously fucked up. Worse, using potions to rupture tendons, blind people, and cripple them was warped. But that's what you got with psychopathic sadists. Fortunately for us, there were a lot of healing and energy potions.

I handed one over to Reaper and he looked relieved.

But just as he was about to use it on Kix, he stopped and stared up at me.

"What if these names don't really represent what these do?" he asked.

"You're right," I said thoughtfully as I let out a slow breath. "Use it on Brazen first."

"What?"

I'd been joking, but Brazen reached out and took the vial from Reaper's hand. He was shaking and barely able to function. Still, he opened the vial and drained it.

He collapsed.

But soon his coloring was coming back.

His eyes snapped open and he choked out, "I guess it *was* a healing potion."

I handed another one to Reaper to give to Kix.

"But if you didn't know it was healing, why..." I stopped and gave him an appraising look.

Every time I jumped to the default reaction of just thinking that Brazen was a douche, he did something to surprise me. He'd taken the elixir because he was protecting his partner. Kix had been too out of it to protest or accept the vial, but Brazen had just enough mental acuity to make the decision to go for it or not.

I gave him an impressed nod.

Then I handed him an energy vial.

"Don't drink it all," I warned. "It'll blow your socks off. Just take a sip."

By now, Kix was rousing and looking decent. Both of their bruises were fading, too.

"Give him some of the energy," I said to Reaper. "I've got enough of these to last us a couple of weeks, but there are more left." My mind went naughty. "Let's fuck with the labels."

Brazen was up now, helping me to switch up the bottles. If any of the bad fae went for any of the healing potions, they'd be suffering something fierce. I couldn't help but grin a bit.

Yeah, I knew I had an evil streak when it came to dealing with bad guys.

But...well...fuck them.

"Couldn't that cause a problem if another torture victim is given one of those potions?" asked Reaper.

"Not if we kill the torturer," answered Kix.

"There are bound to be others," Reaper stated.

"Highly doubtful," I replied, "but we'll ask when we get to him. They don't like to share. But, hey, if there is another one, then we'll come back here and destroy all of this."

Reaper nodded, but I could tell he wasn't happy with this plan.

Satisfied that everything was set, I peeked out of the hut and waved everyone to follow me. We slipped back to the trees, jumping as one when an earsplitting scream sounded from the tent where Methkins was housed. The scream was followed by a sinister laugh.

Mr. Cleary was in serious need of dying.

The look on Reaper's face told me that he agreed with that sentiment.

"Who's in there?" Kix croaked, his throat clearly still dry. "Anyone we know?"

"Timothy Methkins," answered Reaper, keeping his eyes on that tent.

"Meth?" asked Brazen. "What the hell is he doing here? The guy's useless."

Reaper took exception to that comment, spinning on Brazen hotly.

"Were it not for him, we would never have found you."

Brazen held up his hands. "Okay, okay. Sorry I said anything."

"It was pure luck, actually," I pointed out, pushing Reaper back before I explained everything that had happened. A couple minutes later, I said, "So, in a roundabout way, Reap's right. Meth *did* make it possible for us to find you two, but it was more due to his stupidity than anything else."

Reaper shot me a look that included a sneer.

"Don't look at me like that, Reap," I said, giving him my best duck face. "You know I'm right. Meth's a shitty stoner who fucked up just enough to help us out. We *are* going to save him, but don't defend that moron just because you feel we screwed up."

"The man is an innocent," Reaper hissed in response.

"Fair enough," I acquiesced, "but he's still an idiot." Before Reaper could argue, I turned to my other officers and asked, "Now, who wants to kill a fae torture expert?"

I didn't even bother to wait for their hands to go up.

CHAPTER 18

The scream that radiated from the tent where Methkins was being tortured sent a chill up my spine. I couldn't stand that little prick, but I *was* feeling really sorry for him right about now.

"I'm getting him out of there," growled Reaper.

He started to walk toward the edge of the forest, when I saw Temperance heading our way. Brazen clearly saw her, too, because he helped me grab Reaper and pull him back.

We all got down and waited to see what she was going to do.

She walked straight toward us, cut a bit to her right, and then headed down the path that led to the obelisk on this side of reality. That she didn't spot us was a testament to how self-involved she was. Well, that and the fact that we were doing our damndest to remain perfectly still.

"Wait here," I commanded to the three of them.

I followed her just far enough to allow me to spot the obelisk. Then, I waited. If she was going through, we'd make our move to rescue Methkins and teach Cleary a lesson he'd not soon forget. But I wanted to be sure that she was gone before we did anything.

A blink later and she was gone.

When I got back, the other three were up and ready to move.

"I'm taking Reap with me to break out Methkins," I said, setting our strategy. "You two go back to the tent you were having your fun in and build a nice bottle of fun for Mr. Cleary. Make sure you only use ones that already say 'healing' on them, since we messed them about earlier."

My two officers had grins of vengeance on their faces. I couldn't blame them. Cleary had it coming.

"Move," I stated.

Brazen and Kix scurried off, straight ahead of our position. Reaper and I took off to the left and burst through the tent.

The visual was *not* something I wanted to see.

Methkins was seriously fucked up. He had cuts, bruises, teeth missing, and there was blood everywhere. The moment we walked in, Cleary was dropping a hammer on the little wizard's index finger, crushing it. Methkins' agonizing cry was enough to make me want to kill Cleary.

But Reaper got there first.

With a level of anger I'd never seen from my partner, or *anyone* for that matter, Reaper grabbed Cleary by the throat and picked him straight off the ground.

I don't know if this was some kind of reaper-level strength, or if he was just channeling enough rage to win a head-butting contest with a charging rhino, but holy fuck.

Cleary's feet were dangling as he fought to break Reaper's kung-fu grip away from his neck.

I couldn't see that happening.

"Remember that we need him in order to get out of here, Reap," I coaxed my partner as I fumbled for a bottle of healing potion. "Do what you want to him, but don't kill him."

I poured the elixir down Methkins' throat and his eyes slowly opened.

He was still whimpering, though.

Dipshit or not, the guy was messed up really bad. I pushed the hair out of his eyes and gave him more elixir, along with a bit of energy.

It took two and a half bottles to bring him back to full health.

"Shit, man," he said, looking like a terrified child. "That fuckin' hurt."

"I know," I replied as he pushed from the chair and clung to me like a kid clinging to his mother. "Uh..."

"It's people like you," I heard Reaper hissing as he threw Cleary to the ground, "who have caused the world to suffer such pain. You take the helpless and weak and you twist them for your own personal enjoyment."

Cleary was grabbing at his throat while choking. His eyes were full of the same terror he'd undoubtedly seen in countless victims.

Good.

He pushed away from Reaper, but my partner continued stalking him with his eyes.

"I have ferried more souls to the Vortex due to cowards like you than I care to count." Reaper's eyes were glowing so brightly that his sunglasses didn't have a chance at containing them. "I swore that if I ever got the chance, I'd give you a taste of your own medicine."

"No," Cleary pleaded. "Please, no. I'll do anything. I can't handle pain."

"Hey, fuck you, dude," Methkins said, letting go of me. "You're a dick, man."

Cleary was starting to hyperventilate at this point. His eyes glanced at the opening of the tent. He was planning to make a run for it.

"I wouldn't do that," I suggested.

He didn't listen.

He *almost* made it, too, but Reaper was the faster man. Not to mention the stronger one.

My partner, the mostly mild-mannered ex-reaper who preferred *not* to hurt people, had thrown a Superman punch that connected solidly with Cleary's jaw.

The crunch and shriek that followed actually hurt my ears.

I couldn't understand how Cleary remained conscious after that, but he did.

That's when Brazen and Kix arrived. They looked down at the fallen torturer and dived on him. Punches, kicks, and elbows were flying all over the twisted bastard.

"Stop!" I yelled, pulling them away one by one. "We need him to track Temperance, remember?"

I took a bottle of actual healing potion and dumped all but about a quarter of it on the ground. I poured the rest into Cleary's bloodied mouth. He choked a bit. It wasn't enough to fully heal him, but it would suffice to keep him conscious while the pain continued to radiate through his body.

His eyes locked on mine as if asking for more, but I showed him the empty bottle and then dropped it on the floor.

That's when I heard a loud *thwack*, a crunching sound, and the horrible cry that bellowed from Cleary's anguished face.

Looking over, I saw Methkins holding a hammer. He'd crushed Cleary's finger.

Well, at least the scrawny wizard wasn't hugging me anymore.

"Enough," I said, pointing at each of the venomous-faced men on my team. "Help me get him up."

"I need more healing," Cleary begged. "The pain is horrible."

"Sucks, doesn't it?" Brazen snarled.

Kix got face to face with Cleary. "You didn't seem to give a shit when we were feeling like you are now, asshole."

Cleary winced but smartly kept his mouth shut.

"All right," I said, pushing my team back again. Then I looked into Cleary's terrified eyes. "The way I see it, you have two options: you can cooperate with us and I won't let these four gentlemen torture the living hell out of you. Alternatively..." I stopped and just gave him a look that spelled his doom.

"I'll do whatever you want," he said desperately, "but I need healing."

I nodded at him and put my hand out toward Brazen.

He begrudgingly handed me a bottle that said 'healing' on the side. I held it up in front of Cleary but snatched it away when he went to grab it.

"Help us first and you can have it."

"I'll do anything," he said. "Just don't kill me."

"We'll see," I said. Then, "Are you the only torturer or are there others?"

His eyes flashed. "I was assured I was the only one. It's in my contract."

"Contract?" said Brazen. "Who the fuck gets a torture contract?"

"Union rules," Cleary replied with a shrug.

Brazen grimaced. "Who the fuck has a Torturers' Union?"

"The fae, obviously," I answered before Cleary did. "Let's go."

CHAPTER 19

I'd assumed the obelisk would bring us back if we used the same code that we'd used to get here, but something told me that Temperance had traveled elsewhere.

"What's the code to get to where your boss goes?" I asked.

Cleary looked at me and swallowed hard.

I held up the bottle and wiggled it in front of his eyes.

"She'll kill me," Cleary stammered.

"Not if we get to her first," I pointed out. "Of course, if you don't help us, these guys will kill you anyway."

Brazen sweetened the pot further by cracking his knuckles and punching his own hand. Reaper merely took off his shades and showed his high beams.

Cleary swallowed again as his shoulders dropped.

Live by the sword, die by the sword, as the saying goes. The guy had it coming. He was only an inch away from death as it was. All it would take was a little push and he'd be heading toward the Vortex just like many he'd sent there in the past.

"Seven-three-two-six-six," he said, defeated.

"Just to make sure you're not bullshitting us," I informed him, "you'll be joining us on this little trip."

His eyes bulged at that.

"But—"

I crossed my arms, cutting him off. "That's what I thought. Now, I'm assuming you'd like to give us a different number before we step through, Mr. Cleary?"

It was the obvious play for him to give us a fake number. We step through and die, he drains the healing potion and lives. Temperance would never be the wiser. Smart, sure, but also very obvious.

"I'm waiting, Mr. Cleary."

"Six-nine-six-nine-six-nine-one," he muttered.

"Kinky," I said.

He glanced up at me. "Huh?"

"Never mind," I said. Looking at him, he wouldn't have understood anyway. "Put in the numbers."

Reaper tapped away on the keypad as Brazen and Kix grabbed Cleary by his arms, preparing to pull him to the other side with us.

The window opened, revealing an underground area on the other side. I had no clue where it was located, but there were signs of wear and tear on the walls and floors, so it had obviously seen some action.

We walked through.

As soon as we got to the other side, I handed the bottle to Cleary.

He downed it like it was the only glass of water available in Death Valley during the middle of summer.

The look on his face was one of relief...for about three seconds. Then a wave of misery covered it and I could hear the sound of a woeful howl building.

"Throw him back," I commanded Brazen and Kix, but Reaper stepped in and grabbed the broken man first.

"May you die a million deaths," my partner cursed before throwing Cleary back through the portal. "Bastard."

The window closed just as the tormented cry of Cleary began to sound.

There was no way he was going to survive that potion.

"What was in it?" I asked Kix.

"A little bit of everything," he answered. "Well, except for healing and energy, of course."

"Right."

I crouched and looked at the boot prints on the ground. There weren't any deep impressions, but the scuff marks leading to and from the area went in two directions. That would make things a bit tougher.

"Reap," I said, getting back to my feet, "you picking up anything?"

He shook his head.

"I'm not spotting any runes, either," I replied. Then, I looked at Methkins. "I'm assuming you don't see runes in here, right?"

"There aren't any," he replied.

It was the first time he'd given me a simple, easy answer. And the fact that he hadn't mentioned food was amazing.

"All right," I said, looking at each person on my crew. "Brazen, you and Kix take Meth with you and go that way."

"Why do we have to take him?" asked Kix.

"Yeah," Brazen agreed.

"Honestly, I'd rather stay with you," Methkins said, clearly still attaching to me as his protector.

I sighed.

"Can either of you detect runes?" I asked my two trainees pointedly.

They looked at their feet.

I then turned to Methkins.

"And you're going with them because you *can* detect runes," I added. "This isn't a field trip, Meth, and it's not a hotdog run. This is life and death. If you get captured again, you get tortured again. Is that what you want?"

He shook his head dully.

"Then grow a pair, get your mind focused, and do your fucking job. That's your best chance at surviving this little adventure."

At first his eyes were wide, but he slowly began to nod at me.

"Yeah, man," he whispered. "You're right."

I hadn't seen that coming. I was *glad* it did, but it was still a shocker. Even Brazen and Kix were taken aback by the way Methkins had responded.

That was a good thing, though, because I could use it to my advantage.

"Right," I said, glancing up at my two officers. "You two had better do everything you can to protect him, too.

If he gets taken out, you're both screwed because running into runes is not a fun thing."

"Got it," Brazen said, clearly recognizing that my little speech was intended to benefit Methkins. "We'll cover him."

Methkins breathed a sigh of relief at that.

"*Are these working now?*" I asked through the connector.

Everyone nodded.

"*Whew. Good. That means we're not in another dimensional box.*"

"*A what?*" asked Kix.

"*The place with the tents wasn't real...sort of,*" I said with a shrug. "*Ask Meth, I'm sure he can explain it better than I can.*"

"*It's a magical realm that gets setup by a powerful wizard dude...or chick...*" Methkins began as they headed off.

I tuned the volume down and blew out a relieved breath.

"You did well, Piper," Reaper said aloud.

"Thanks," I replied. "Same to you." I then gave him the once-over. "Oh, and you're a madman when you're pissed off."

"Sorry."

"For what?" I said with a laugh. "I fucking loved it."

CHAPTER 20

$\mathcal{T}$he tunnel should have been covered with cameras, but the fae likely doubted anyone would ever come down here other than them. Still, arrogant or not, only an idiot avoided taking at least *some* precautions.

Everything was going swell until we turned a corner and found ourselves looking at a bunch of fae security guards.

I tried to jump back, but it was too late.

"You there," yelled one of the guards as I pulled out my gun and fired off a Death Nail at her.

She gurgled her last, but that only resulted in a siren coming on and lights flashing down the tunnels.

"*What the fuck's going on?*" asked Brazen through the connector.

"*Piper has been spotted,*" Reaper replied in a calm voice. I gave him a look. "What?" he said aloud. "*I wasn't spotted.*"

"Get ready to fight, Reap," I commanded. "Do some of that same shit you did to Cleary."

He didn't reply, but when the first guard came around the corner, I had to cringe at the punch Reaper unleashed at him. The guy didn't have a chance.

I took out the second one with a couple of shots to the chest. Death Nails did a fine job in single shots, but two or more working together were even faster at accomplishing their mission.

"Back off," commanded a woman's voice that sounded a lot like Temperance.

The sound of retreating footsteps could be heard.

"This is Minister Temperance Q'Lau of the Fae Consortium," she stated firmly. "You have trespassed on private property and it is well within my rights to have you summarily executed."

"Shove it up your ass," I replied. "You're the bitch who's been starting riots in the city and we know it."

It went quiet for a few moments.

Finally, she replied, "Pity."

That's when an empiric slid across the floor in front of me and Reaper.

"Run!"

We got about ten steps before the world went wobbly.

My ears were ringing like a motherfucker and my vision was blurred, but I could still sense the bodies that were surrounding us.

"*That wasn't intended to kill us,*" Reaper said through the connector, though he sounded like he was struggling to get the words out.

Hell, I was struggling to understand them.

"*Nope,*" I replied as we were being dragged down the hall. "*Concussion Empiric. That shit is not fun.*"

We sounded like a couple of drunks.

"You guys okay?" asked Kix.

"Captured," was my only response.

"Shit," said Kix.

"Yep," I agreed. *"Just keep on with your mission to put a stop to Temperance. I'm going to go to sleep now."*

"I could only understand about half of what you said," informed Kix.

It sounded clear enough to me when I was talking.

"We'll get you out," Brazen stated emphatically.

"No," Reaper replied, taking the lead as I felt the world slipping away. *"It's more important that you stop Temperance than it is for us to be saved."*

"Reap," I heard Brazen say an instant before the world went black, *"I love ya like a sister, but fuck you."*

CHAPTER 21

When I finally came to, I found myself strapped to a table that was inclined at about a forty-five-degree angle. There were wires connected to me that ran to what looked like a battery. To my left was an identical table that held Reaper. His shades were off, but his eyes were closed.

The rest of the room was dark and dank. Various instruments of torture were laid out and they didn't look all that fun. What was it with these people?

The entire ordeal, including what had happened to Brazen, Kix, and Methkins, was giving me an entirely new perspective on the fae. I'd always thought them to be prim, proper, and above the warp-mindedness that seemed a natural part of the supernatural community as a whole. It was turning out that they were the sickest fuckers of the bunch. At least the lot down here, anyway. Seeing that Temperance *was* the fae leader, though, I couldn't help but think that this maniacally villainous shit that was happening was either the fae status quo or it was just a release of all that pent-up frustration of being the butt of jokes all these years. People considered fae to be tricksters, and they teased them about that relentlessly. I know I did, anyway. But maybe the only trick they'd been playing was the one that made them appear to be the quiet kid in class. You know the one—mouth shut, but eyes bright and studying, always surveying and taking notes. Yeah, she was calm and thoughtful on the surface, but behind that facade was a mind that planned the punishment of everyone who'd ever done her wrong. The primary difference was that this fae seemed to be taking the step from thinking about it to doing it.

"Reap," I croaked and then coughed. My throat was beyond parched. "Reap!"

He didn't budge.

I tried again through my connector. *"Reap!"*

His eyes snapped open and he began coughing even worse than I had. Finally, he caught his breath and began looking around the room, settling on the restraints holding him in place.

"Nice place," he joked. "I take it we didn't win the firefight."

"You okay?"

He nodded. "You?"

"I've been better," I answered, my head pounding from the concussion that damn Empiric had left me with. "Wasn't expecting to get flashed."

"Yeah." Then he mouthed, "The others?"

"Just use your connector," I said, *"and I haven't checked."* I went to hold up a finger, but then I remembered I was still strapped down. *"Brazen, you there?"*

"*Yeah,*" he replied. "*We've found a back room that has a bunch of crates and such. There are weapons and potions and all sorts of fun shit in here.*"

"*Anything you can rig up to blow it all to hell?*"

"*Definitely,*" he replied. "*Methkins is working on a few runes for that right now, actually.*" There was a pause. "*I think being tortured like we were flicked a switch on in his head. Never seen him work like this before.*"

"*Good,*" I said, thankful that the stoner wizard had turned a corner, even if only for now; on the other hand, I didn't really give a shit because I was certainly going to be tortured myself soon. "*Keep on that and then get out of here. That's an order.*"

"*Fuck off, Piper,*" Brazen replied. "*As soon as we're done here, we're coming for you.*"

"*No, Officer Brazen,*" I shot back, "*you are not. Your job is to—*"

"*Hello?*" he interrupted. "*You still there, Piper? I can't hear you very well. You're breaking up.*"

"*Asshole.*"

"*Count on it,*" he affirmed. "*See you soon. Brazen out.*"

Okay, so I admit that a part of me was relieved that he was planning to attempt to rescue me and Reaper, but I was also pissed. Protecting the masses was more important than protecting us. It was part of the oath we took as cops. Granted, Reaper and I were Retrievers, so we had a different oath that didn't include the *protecting others* crap, but Brazen and Kix weren't full-fledged Retrievers yet. They were still cops. Their duty was to the people, not to us.

Then again, blowing up this place *was* a grand step in

protecting the people, even if all five PPD officers perished in the process.

"*He'll never listen, you know,*" Reaper noted, closing his eyes again. "*He's too much like you.*"

"What?" I scoffed aloud.

He opened one eye. "Tell me he's not."

I couldn't.

The truth was that Brazen and I had a lot in common. More than I cared to admit, in fact. He was brash, mouthy, tough, good at fighting, and had that same shoot-first-and-ask-questions-later process of handling criminals that I had. The primary differences between us were in the realm of personal hygiene and clothing choices. Now, I couldn't speak for what he may have worn on Friday nights, but I also didn't want my mind to go there...ever.

"Ugh," I said finally.

Reaper grinned slightly at that.

"We always dislike the ones who remind us of who we are, Piper."

"You don't remind me of myself at all, Reap, and I'm not really loving you at the moment."

His grin widened.

"I'm more like Kix, I think," he admitted. "We are both filled with empathy. Our first instinct is to heal and protect. This is why you and I make a good team, just as Brazen and Kix do."

"Riiight," I said with a laugh. "Kix is a real humanitarian. And when you say 'heal and protect,' do you mean like you did to Cleary?" His grin faded almost instantly. "I've never seen you like that before, Reap. Kind of freaked me out, if I'm being honest."

Reaper's eyes were open again, glowing brightly. He was scanning the floor and his face had reddened a fair amount. Obviously, bringing up the late, great Mr. Cleary had reignited a flame of rage.

"The man had it coming," he muttered through clenched teeth. "Not only was he a monster, his evilness infected others…including me."

"Yeah, I kind of noticed that."

Reaper slowly turned to stare into my eyes. It wasn't the kind of stare that gave you the warm and fuzzies, either.

"If you had seen one-millionth of what I've seen over the years, Piper," he seethed, "you'd have made me look like a saint in that tent with Cleary."

I inclined my head.

He was right, of course.

Yes, I was immortal, but I'd only been around a tiny fraction of the time Reaper had been. In my young life, I'd seen enough and been subjected to enough to make me jaded and generally irritable. But Reap had to stand idly by as people suffered until death set in. He wasn't allowed to interfere, regardless of how much he might have longed to. His job was to wait for them to die, and then he could take their fractured souls and ferry them to their final resting place in the Vortex.

There were undoubtedly many Mr. Clearys in Reaper's past. I only had a few to ignite my deepest feelings of angst, and that was enough to make my powers superhuman. I couldn't even fathom what happened in Reaper's mind at seeing these things in his corporeal state.

Well, I suppose I *could*, now that I'd seen him in action.

It wasn't pleasant.

"You're right, Reap," I apologized. "Sorry."

He closed his eyes again and looked away.

"It's okay," he said finally. "I know you better than you know yourself, Piper. You don't mean to spew acid at me. You're just protecting yourself from getting too close. It's the same for Brazen."

I frowned at that observation, but I knew he was right.

Any time I had allowed myself to get close to anyone over the years, it turned out negatively—boyfriends, fellow officers, regular friends...nothing ever lasted.

"Thanks for making me feel even more depressed than I already was at the thought of being tortured, Reap," I mumbled. "You're a real pal."

His grin returned.

Then the door opened and Temperance walked into the room.

Behind her was a very determined-looking Mr. Cleary.

Much to my surprise, Reaper said, "Aw, fuck."

CHAPTER 22

$\mathcal{N}$ ow, I *knew* we left that guy for dead, and I was certain that the mixture of all those potions had to have put him over the top...or was that under the bottom? I guess that would teach us to check for a pulse before making assumptions in the future... assuming there was a future.

"*Hey, Brazen,*" I said in a direct connection, "*remember all that shit I said about keeping to the mission and not coming after us?*"

"*Yeah.*"

"*Fuck that noise. Our pal Cleary is still alive and he doesn't look happy.*"

"*Shit. On our way.*"

I couldn't imagine ever thinking that hearing Brazen say he was on his way would make me feel a sense of relief. Usually, it'd bring on a bout of nausea. But I guess Reaper was right about the man. He *was* a lot like me, and that meant we had a fighting chance of getting out of this before we were mangled too badly.

"I have to say, Officer Shaw," Temperance said as she leaned back against the wall with her arms crossed, "I wouldn't have expected to see a Retriever down here."

"Yeah?" I replied while keeping tabs on Cleary's preparations out of the corner of my eye. "Well, what are ya gonna do, ya know?"

"Oh, I'm going to let Mr. Cleary torture you both thoroughly," she replied sweetly. "He was rather adamant about being allowed to work you both over. It seems that you nearly killed him."

Cleary snarled in our direction.

"I don't suppose an apology would help?" I asked hopefully.

Another snarl answered that question.

"Ah well," I sighed. "What the hell if you can't take a joke, ya know?"

Temperance smirked.

"It's nice to see a tough lady, Officer Shaw."

"Just call me Piper, yeah?" I said. "That 'Officer Shaw' crap makes me feel too proper. I'm *not* proper."

"No," Temperance agreed, "you're not. And that's what I like about you. You're tough, resilient, and smart. Ladies like us need to stick together."

I blinked at her. "Huh?"

"I didn't mean *us*, specifically," she corrected while motioning between herself and me. "I was speaking metaphorically."

"Yeah, okay." I shook my head, grimacing. "So, what the fuck are you talking about, then?"

She gave me a look that made it clear she wasn't a fan of my using that kind of language with her. I guess

I'd forgotten she was the leader of all fae. Not that I really gave a shit in the grand scheme of things, but in my current position a little tact would probably be wise.

"I'm in the unique position of being able to stop Mr. Cleary here from exacting any pain on you two," Temperance replied, pushing off the wall and stepping between the sadist and us. "He's simply dying to dive right in and get to work, but there are certain things that I need in order to take my plan a step further."

Okay, so she wanted to play the game with us. That was cool with me. I knew damn well it wouldn't stop her from opening the gate for Cleary once she got what she wanted, but it'd delay the inevitable and hopefully give Brazen, Kix, and Methkins time to get to us before things got too rough.

I was going to direct connect with Reaper, but he'd already pointed out that he knew me pretty well by now.

"I'm listening," I said finally.

"You liberated the three others who were in the dimensional box," she said. "Where are they?"

"We sent them back to base to get reinforcements," I lied.

"Good, good," she said, her face shining even more beautifully than before. "That will pull resources away from the precinct."

"So?"

"So our goal is to take over your base, Officer..." She smiled. "Sorry, I mean Piper."

"Is that why you were speaking with Keller?" I asked, knowing it wasn't the wisest course of action, but I had to do it. When she blanched, I added, "I'm talking about the guy who set up that dimensional box from before."

The unexpected slap that connected with my face a moment later hurt like hell. Temperance was apparently quite strong. Worse, she had nails that felt like they were made of steel, and they raked my cheek rather nicely.

"Hit them," she commanded Cleary.

He didn't need to be told twice. The sadistic fae spun a couple of knobs on a device that was connected to the battery linked to us by wires.

Reaper and I began convulsing like mad.

I'd touched runes before that shocked me, and I'd even been hit by energy pulses fired at me from the fingers of mages, but those were child's play compared to this flow of joy. I could damn well feel my eyes rolling up into my head and I thought certain I was going to crack my teeth due to how hard I was clenching my jaw.

Both Reaper and I were yelling uncontrollably until the electricity halted.

My head lulled forward for a second as I heaved in pain.

"Ouch," I whimpered, and I wasn't someone who typically whimpered. But, fuck, that hurt. "What say we *don't* do that again?"

Temperance grabbed my face and roughly pulled it up to look into hers.

"Don't *ever* mention that traitor's name to me again," she asserted.

"Keller?" I said and then my eyes went wide. "Sorry! I was just making sure that's who you meant."

Her stare was laced with very bad intentions.

"He's a dick, anyway," I said, hoping that would appease her.

Her eyes flashed for a moment and then she let me go.

"What do you know of him?" she asked, taking a step back.

I felt drool pouring from my lips, but I mumbled the best I could.

"He killed a lot of normals in the late eighties. He also led a revolt against the PPD, but he failed. Now, he's back to his old tricks." I struggled to look up at the fae. "And he's known for screwing over people who he's supposed to be partnered with. I'm assuming he's done that to you as well?"

She glanced away, nodding.

"May I send another course through them now, ma'am?" asked Cleary.

"Not yet," Temperance warned.

I sighed in relief at that, even though I was certain it was only going to be a minor reprieve. Still, I'd take what I could get.

"You're the reaper who was assigned to work with the PPD a few years ago, yes?" Temperance asked Reaper, turning her attention to him. "I'd heard of you, but your eyes were never glowing in any of the pictures I've seen."

"They were doctored in my photographs," he answered raggedly. "I cannot explain why my superiors found that to be necessary, but they apparently did."

"Apparently," Temperance replied. "What can *you* tell me of Keller?"

Reaper licked his lips. "Only that he is a narcissistic

megalomaniac who thrives on discord and chaos. He longs for power and he believes he's a god."

"Sounds about right," Temperance said. "Do either of you know how to defeat him?"

Reaper and I glanced at each other and then shook our heads in unison.

Temperance sneered and flicked her hand at Cleary.

The energy streamed through us again.

CHAPTER 23

*P*ain will make you do things you never thought you'd do. For some people, they'd beg and plead and tell you anything you wanted to know. Others would shrivel into nothing and just suffer, waiting for the darkness to come. For someone like Reaper, it just made him go completely cold and businesslike. Me? I became a flat-out cantankerously boisterous pain in the ass.

"Crack us with it again, you fuckin' shit stain," was what I babbled as soon as the third wave of electricity diminished. "You're all tough when we're tied up, Cleary the Queery." I cackled at my little joke. "That's your new name, Cleary the Queeryyyyyyy!"

I hadn't actually sung out that last part. It only sounded that way because Cleary spun the goddamn dial on me again.

Temperance almost instantly told him to cut it off, though.

"Awwwww," I slurred. "Mommy won't wet da widdle

baby pway!"

In response, I got another nice smack across the face. It burned because Temperance's pinky nail slit my eyelid. But that just fed my insanity even more.

"You hit like a girl," I said, laughing as the blood dripped into my eye. "You *look* like a boy, but you hit like a girlllllllllll!"

Another jolt, this time authorized by the leader of the fae.

It stopped about five seconds later.

"Are you finished?" Temperance asked. "Or would you like some more?"

"I can do this all day, bitch," I replied, though I doubted it sounded anything like that due to my lips being numb. "Let me out of this chair and I'll fuck you up."

Temperance stood up and shook her head at me. She then walked over to Reaper and ran one of her nails down his face seductively.

He didn't budge.

"A reaper must have seen many things," she said in a seductive way.

"Hey," I blurted like a drunken fool, "how come I get slapped around and he gets all the lovey talk? I'm not gay, but I'll try playing for the other side if you'll quit smacking the shit outta meeeeeeee!"

Honestly, I had to learn to keep my mouth shut.

But I couldn't.

The longer I kept this stupid fae and her asshole torture guy going, the more chance Reaper and I had to survive. This assumed that Brazen, Kix, and Methkins would be able to mount a decent rescue effort, of course.

One thing was for sure, if we got out of this damn situation, we *weren't* going to get caught again.

"*Are you guys getting close at all?*" I asked Brazen through a direct connection. "*We're getting our asses kicked in here.*"

"*We just dropped three guards and had to pull them into a dark room,*" he replied.

"*Did you just say you dropped down in front of three guards and pulled them off in a dark room?*" I asked, thinking I *had* to have heard that wrong.

"*I absolutely didn't,*" Brazen replied in a tight voice. "*You're obviously delirious. I think we're getting close. This place just has a lot of twists and turns.*"

"*Follow the screams,*" I told him.

"*Hang in there, Piper.*"

"*Yeah, yeah, yeah.*"

I gave a quick glance over at Cleary. He was watching as Temperance held a seductive dialog with my partner. Reaper remained silent the entire time, but I could tell that Cleary was *not* pleased with the game his boss was playing.

Jealousy?

That was my bet.

And that meant it was time to fuck with him some.

"What's the matter, Cleary?" I deadpanned. "Don't like it when the boss wants to wrap her tits around another guy's cock?"

The look he gave me was priceless. It was a mixture of hate, distaste, and downright fascination. He probably thought that it wasn't ladylike of me to speak in such a filthy fashion.

JOHN P. LOGSDON & CHRISTOPHER P. YOUNG

"Oh, I'm sorry," I said, opening my good eye a little wider. "Was that too graphic for you?"

"Quite," he replied.

"My bad," I said and then spit out some blood. "Let me try again. Are you worried that your boss may want to toss my partner's salad while giving him the best tug job he's ever haddddddddd!?!?!"

Temperance spun on him and yelled, "Stop!"

He did, but his glare remained.

I just laughed right in his face. It was a forced laugh. Agonizing and difficult, but I couldn't let him get the upper hand.

"It really bugs the shit out of you doesn't it, Cleary the Queery?" I said, fighting to maintain my consciousness. "What I'm not quite sure of, though, is whether you're jealous of Temperance, or Reaper."

"What are you saying?" Cleary hissed, sneaking a peek at Temperance, likely making sure his voice wasn't loud enough to bother her.

My shrug in response was weak, but I managed. "Just that I think maybe the real jealousy stems from the fact that *you're* the one who wants to play a game of hide the beef with my partnerrrrrrr!"

Temperance turned again on Cleary, but this time she smacked *him* across the face. He yelped like the wimp that I knew him to be. It made me giggle.

"Yay," I wheezed. "One point for our side. Eh, Reap?"

Reaper gazed over at me, shaking his head.

"You're crazy, you know that?"

"Yup."

A knock came at the door as Temperance was reading

126

the riot act to Cleary. She didn't answer until she was certain that her main torturer was prepared to control himself. Based on the look on his face, he wouldn't touch that dial no matter what I said from that point on, at least while she was in the room.

The knock sounded again, this time much more insistently.

"What is it?" Temperance yelled out, opening the door. A young man on the other side kneeled immediately. "Get up, get up," she complained. "Why are you disturbing me?"

"You asked to be notified when the PPD turned up at the main Faeland gate, ma'am," he said, keeping his eyes affixed to the ground in front of her. "There are many officers on site, and they have a warrant."

"Perfect," she replied. Then she turned back to Cleary. "Do whatever you want with them, but make sure they're dead within the hour." She pointed firmly at him. "One hour, or you'll be dead too."

Then she gave us one last look and walked out.

Cleary's face was so full of joy in that moment that it was as if he'd just been handed his first present on Christmas morning.

"Looks like you're in charge now," I said.

"Yes," he cheered, "and you're going to suffer an incredible amount before you die."

"You can torture us and kill us and..." I paused. "Well, that's about it, I suppose. But just remember something..." I squinted at him as best I could. "To me, Cleary the Queery, you'll always be a big fat pussyyyyyyyyyyyy!"

Okay, that time I started singing it, but he spun the dials after a few seconds to help me carry the note.

CHAPTER 24

You know that weird person in your family who makes you uncomfortable whenever they show up at holiday parties? The one who says things that make you cringe? If you don't think you have someone like that in your family, it's you.

Anyway, that's how I felt about Brazen.

Or, I should say, that's how I used to feel about Brazen, until he kicked down that motherlovin' door and cracked Cleary on the back of his head with the butt of his revolver.

We were in the middle of a buzz-cycle, but Kix quickly spun the knobs down.

"Temperance and her goons are going to try and hit the station," I wheezed. "Somebody contact the chief and warn him."

"I've already tried," Reaper replied, sounding even worse than me. "The signal isn't going through for some reason."

"Mine won't connect either," Kix said.

Brazen shook his head also.

"Shit."

Methkins rushed over to undo our bindings.

Who knew these three could be so effective when they really applied themselves?

"Thanks," I groaned, falling face first onto the floor.

It was sad, but my face smacking the ground was the best thing I'd felt all day.

Reaper collapsed beside me a moment later.

"Get them healing potions, quick," commanded Brazen, taking control of the situation. "Wait! Make sure that's actually healing and not one of our concoctions."

"How?" asked Kix.

"Give some to that fucker."

I assumed "that fucker" was Cleary. My assumption proved correct when I heard Mr. Torturer say, "What happened?" a few seconds later. This was followed by, "Oh no…"

As Kix knelt down to pour some of the healing potion into my mouth, I saw Brazen dragging Cleary over to the magical electric chair that Reaper had been strapped to.

Cleary fought, but he was no match for a werebear, even one in human form.

Warmth filled my being and my head began to clear. Reaper's eyes were picking up in intensity again as well. Neither of us was one hundred percent yet, but at least we were able to sit up now.

"You don't understand," Cleary was begging. "I was just doing my job."

That was one excuse that pissed me off more than any other.

I chugged another bottle of healing potion and waited to feel wonderful again. It didn't take long. We'd likely have to sleep for a few days to recover from all this potion, but for now the mixture of anger and adrenaline would keep us going.

"Please, just let me go…"

"Shut up, you piece of shit," I hissed at him. "You should have died last time we left you for dead." I blinked at my own words as everyone squinted at me. "Anyway, we're not making that mistake twice."

Then, I had an idea.

I walked over to him and yanked his pants down. It was easy since they were the kind that just had an elastic band.

"What are you doing?" he said with a face of horror.

"Don't worry, idiot," I replied tersely. "I'm not going to take advantage of you." Then I glanced down at his little pal. "Dainty. Are all fae hung like crickets or is it just you?"

"Uh…"

"Honestly, it looks like a frightened turtle." I then glanced at Reaper. "That wasn't intended as a slight against Agnes, I assure you."

I'm pretty sure my partner rolled his eyes. It was difficult to tell in this lighting, especially with his high beams on.

"Okay," I announced, "now I just need a knife and some pickle juice."

"What?" asked a terrified Cleary.

I turned to grin at my crew but then remembered they were all men. The looks on their faces all screamed "NOT COOL!"

I sighed.

"Never mind," I said while turning to Kix. "Just give him some of that fun potion."

"I'm not going near a naked dude," Kix said as he threw me a bottle. "You're the one who pulled his pants down."

I shrugged and cracked open the bottle.

"No, no, no...please!"

"Would you rather I find that knife and pickle juice?" I asked with a tilt of my head. He whimpered. "It's not fun being on the other side of the torture, is it, asshole?"

He was visibly shaking.

"All right, all right," I said, closing up the bottle with a grunt. "I won't make you drink the potion." I shook my head at him and yanked his pants back up. "Honestly, you're such a pussy."

Cleary sighed in relief.

"Reaper," I said over my shoulder, "I believe you know what to do."

And he did.

The room nearly went dark when my partner spun the dial that unleashed energetic happiness. Cleary screamed so hard that I thought he would blow out his vocal chords.

Reaper shut it back off after a few seconds.

"Sucks, doesn't it?" I chided the sobbing man. "Too bad we can't hang around for more fun, though. We have to kill your boss and such."

"Please...I'll do anything..."

"I know," I said, whipping out my gun and pointing it at him. "Unfortunately, we can't risk you surviving again."

"No, please!"

"Don't take it personally, dickhead," I said with a cold stare. "I'm just doing my job."

Two Death Nails later, Mr. Cleary was no more.

CHAPTER 25

*W*e walked back out into the corridor, prepared for anything. I was happily prepared take a bullet over being subjected to any further torture. I was done with that shit.

The place appeared to be empty, which kind of sucked because it meant we couldn't use anyone to help us get out of this joint.

"I guess I should have asked Cleary how to get out of here, huh?"

"We already know," Brazen said, taking point.

He took off at a rate that a werebear shouldn't be able to move. Honestly, one look at the guy and you'd think he lived on donuts and pizza. To be fair, a dozen donuts sounded pretty damn good right about then. I didn't dare mention that, though, since it'd probably start Methkins off on a rant about wanting hotdogs. Damn it…hotdogs *did* sound good.

We cut a corner and saw a stream of fae heading up a

135

flight of stairs. I didn't recall seeing that exit when we arrived here. Obviously, there was more magic involved.

Fucking Keller.

One fae spotted us and pointed.

I didn't even hesitate this time, and neither did Kix and Brazen. We had our guns out in a flash, Death Nails flying everywhere. Even Reaper was in on the act, running his fingers over his tattoo and launching fireballs.

It was great...unless you were a fae.

They tried to retaliate, but we'd hit them too fast.

But that's when an explosion rocked us all, throwing everyone toward the far wall, next to the obelisk.

The tunnel we'd just exited caved in.

"That'd be my spell launching off," Methkins groaned. "Shit, man."

On the plus side, the fae were busily crushing each other in a mad attempt to get out. They'd all but forgotten about us.

"Is that it for the explosions?" asked Kix as he rubbed his head. "That seemed kind of tame for all the stuff that was in that room."

"That was tame?" I asked.

"Two more coming, dude," Methkins replied.

"We'll never survive two more of those," Kix grunted.

"Neither will they," Brazen pointed out while motioning to the mass of crazed fae. "Besides, we have to die sometime."

"Fuck that," I said, standing up and entering the original code into the obelisk the guards had used when transporting Methkins. It was either going to take us to the dimensional box or we'd end up back in Faeland. It didn't matter to me. We could figure out the next steps from there. Sadly, the damn thing didn't work. "Shit."

"What's the matter?" asked Reaper.

"It's not working."

"Makes sense," noted Brazen. "If *that* was working, why would they bother with the stairs?"

"Let me see it," Methkins said, pushing me out of the way.

I stood back as he frantically drew symbols all around the obelisk. I'd never seen a wizard work so fast. Maybe shock therapy really *did* help this guy?

The second explosion hit.

It was worse than the first, but we only felt the shockwave of it. The fae were the ones who took the brunt of the falling rock.

Not pretty.

"We've only got about a minute before the last one goes off," Methkins said, not adding "dude" or "man" to his statement. "Get ready with that code, dude."

Ah, there it was.

After a few more flicks of his hand, the obelisk began to glow.

"Now!"

I tapped in the code and a window opened.

One by one, we all jumped through, ending up in Faeland an instant before the ground shook something fierce and the window closed.

The third explosion had finished the job.

CHAPTER 26

The only thing I wanted to do at that moment was lie down on the grass and sleep. Yes, I was physically healed, but my brain was still freaking out over what I'd just been through. Besides, potions were notorious for tiring you out.

"Stay where you are," a stern voice said from behind us.

I shot a glance over my shoulder and saw that we were standing in front of about twenty fae.

None of them appeared to be armed.

"Or what?" I asked as I turned around with the rest of my crew. "Are you going to give us all fresh hairdos and makeovers?"

The guy who had warned us not to move furrowed his brow at my comment.

"What?"

"Well, it's not like you have any weapons," I pointed out. Then I held up my gun. "Oh, and we *do*. So, seeing that your culture is one that focuses primarily on beauty, I figured that hair styling and makeup application would be your superpower." I sniffed. "I thought you were tricksters, but so far I'm not seeing it."

The guy put his hand on his hip and glared.

"Do you have any idea how racist that is?"

I shrugged. "It's only racist if I claim it to be a negative thing. I mean, let's be honest, your community *is* gorgeous, right? Would you *rather* I called you a bunch of tricksters?"

"I suppose that's true," he replied, pursing his lips as the others with him nodded. "Still, the way you said it made it very clear that you meant it in a derogatory fashion."

Okay, fair enough. I did. But I only did that because I was trying to throw them off their game.

It was clearly working.

"I apologize, then," I said with a slight bow before pointing my gun at him. "Now, get your hands up or I'll shoot you."

He smiled.

Why did he smile?

"Any idea why he's smiling?" I said out of the corner of my mouth. "I don't like that he's smiling."

"No clue," replied Brazen. "It *is* kind of freaky, though."

"Yep," agreed Kix. "Freaky."

Right when I was about to question Mr. Pretty regarding his sudden demeanor change, a mass of weapons appeared out of nowhere. Every one of the fae was holding a menacing piece of arsenal.

"Fucking tricksters!" I yelled as I dived toward the nearest tree.

The place was lit up with ammunition. It was cutting into the tree I was hiding behind, causing me to kick my feet around in the dirt while covering my ears.

Reaper had grabbed Methkins and dived behind a large rock. Brazen and Kix were crawling as fast as they could to find cover as well.

"Damn it," I hissed to myself as I reached out and started firing Death Nails in the general direction of the fae mob. "Eat Nails, fuckers!"

"*Reap,*" I said through the connector, "*stun them or fireball them or whatever the hell you can do!*"

"*Already on it,*" he said as a blast of energy flew from his fingers.

Multiple shrieks and grunts sounded from the direction of the fae. That gave me time to roll out and start firing again. Brazen and Kix were also clicking off round after round.

It didn't take long before the field had been cleared.

"Son of a bitch." I panted as I stood up and stomped on the ground. "Those bastards really *are* tricksters."

"I could've told you that," Brazen said as he walked over. "This isn't topside, Piper. You're in the Netherworld, remember? You may be queen of the Retrievers, but this ain't your station. Kix and I have been walking this beat for years." He nodded at Kix. "We'll bow to you topside without question, but if you want to get through this alive, you might want to listen to us."

I wanted to argue the point with him, but he was right. Still, a cop was a cop, right? And didn't Reaper and I originally save their sorry asses from being tortured to death? If they were so great at the run-and-gun game down here, how come it took two topside Retrievers to break them out?

Regardless, they *did* know the Netherworld better than us.

"Fair enough," I said with a lot of effort, "you guys take point, but don't treat us like a couple of rookies or I'll—"

"Slice my nuts open and dip them in pickle juice?" Brazen finished for me. "I know."

With that, he turned and started walking.

"Do I say that a lot or something?" I asked Reaper via direct connection. *"I don't think I say that a lot."*

"I believe it's more the spirit of the thing, Piper," he replied, grinning. *"You often threaten to destroy testicles in interesting ways."*

"So? Take away someone's favorite toy and they start to cooperate. Basic psychology."

He gave me a funny look.

"I contacted the chief," announced Kix. "It seems that the cops who arrived at the front gate were attacked and suffered quite a few casualties."

"That means they'll be hitting the precinct soon," I cursed.

"They're already there," Kix replied.

We broke into a run.

$\mathcal{O}$ur weapons were drawn when we hit the front gates, but there was no way we were going to make it through the mass of fae standing there. Fortunately, they were all facing away from us, looking out at the city.

"Let me handle this," said Brazen, holding out his hand to slow us down.

He continued until he was close enough to yell out at them.

"All right," he called out, causing the group of fae to turn and look at him, "we're from the Paranormal Police Department and we're on official business. We need to exit Faeland now and we expect your full cooperation. Failure to cooperate will result in…"

Brazen trailed off as the fae moved to either side of the gate.

By the time we reached Brazen's spot, there was a wide expanse for us to walk out to freedom.

"Holy shit, Moses," I said, checking to see if Brazen was holding up a staff. "How'd you manage that?"

"I don't have a fucking clue," he mumbled, frowning.

It didn't matter anyway. They were letting us go, so we high-tailed it out of there.

Almost.

Just as we were passing through the exit, a gorgeous man stepped in our way. He had his hands up at shoulder height, showing that he meant us no harm. But I kept my gun ready, just in case.

"My name is Minos Pellan," he said. "I am the leader of the peace movement in this community, as well as a second-level Chancellor on the general circuit."

"Okay?" I said, squinting at him. "What's up, Minos?"

"Temperance has acted beyond the will of the people in our area. We do not support what she is doing."

"What exactly *is* she doing?" asked Reaper.

Minos took a deep breath. "Her mind has been tainted by an evil mage. He subjected most of the council, in fact, but some of us held steadfast and were imprisoned." He looked over the crowd. "I'm only here because these fine people freed me and the others."

"Yeah," I said, glancing past the gate. "Well, it seems like Keller double-crossed Temperance, but she's already tasted power. She's attacking the PPD precinct right now, in fact."

"We know."

I gave him a look. "Swell."

"How may we be of assistance?"

"Uh…" I stammered. "I…uh…we could use a car."

"And some hotdogs," said Methkins.

We all turned and stared at him for a second. Then I shrugged my shoulders.

"Yeah," I agreed. "Some hotdogs would be cool, too."

Unfortunately, there were no hotdogs available, but we jumped into the car that pulled up a minute later and sped back toward the precinct.

The city center was still in tatters, but Kix was taking side streets to avoid congestion. It was a good thing he was driving. I didn't know these streets as well as he did. If I had been behind the wheel, we'd be sitting in gridlock.

"Don't get too close," I warned as we started getting near the station. "We're already going to be facing down more fae than we can probably handle. My hope is that we'll be able to position ourselves and take them out from hiding spots. That'll make them panic."

Reaper looked at me thoughtfully. "Guerrilla warfare?"

I nodded.

"*Chief,*" I connected, making sure everyone in the car was linked into the conversation, "*we're here. How are you holding up?*"

"*They haven't gotten through yet, but it's getting close,*" he replied. "*Pecker has put up the standard field and he has someone helping him to keep the locks on something called a 'running configuration.' I don't know what in blazes he's talking about, though.*"

"*It just means that the lock system is constantly changing access codes,*" Pecker chimed in, obviously picking up on the call. My guess was that the chief had added him. "*Agnes is handling that, actually.*"

Reaper smiled for a moment, and then his face went

stone cold. Clearly, he'd just realized that his beloved turtle would have been safer at home.

"*Hang in there, guys,*" I said. "*We're going to start picking them off from out here. We'll keep to the shadows and stir panic, if we can.*"

"*Good plan,*" replied the chief.

The area was pretty packed with fae and Temperance was obviously at the front of that pack, but we couldn't see her from here. There were a few fae goons scanning the area as well. My guess was that they were tasked with making sure they didn't get flanked.

They'd have to be the first to go.

"Okay, guys," I said as I continued looking for locations to attack from, "we're going to need to split up. Each of you has to find a well-hidden spot. Take careful aim and pick off fae one at a time. Don't just unleash on them or they'll catch your position." I continued talking as I made sure my Death Nails were fully stocked. "Three shots and then move."

"What about me?" asked Methkins.

Honestly, I hadn't considered him in this plan. Wizards weren't known for using weaponry, and Methkins didn't really look like the type who would be useful in a hand-to-hand situation. My thought was to just tell him to scoot and we'd send him a coupon for hotdogs or something by way of a thank you.

But the look on his face told me he was in it to win it.

"Can you shoot a gun?" I asked.

"Never have," he said, glancing down at my weapon with a face of worry, "but I'm willing to try."

"Sorry," I replied, "no time for on-the-job training here. Just come with me and do as I say, agreed?"

He nodded firmly.

"No, wait," Reaper interjected. "I think it'd be better if he and I worked together. I have an idea, but I'll need genuine magic to accomplish it."

"Fine with me," I said, and then I looked at each of my crew in turn. "Let's fuck with their heads, boys."

CHAPTER 28

*O*nce everyone called in their position as being set, I was ready to give the word to commence firing. It wasn't exactly the way I wanted to handle this, but five against however many fae were out there wasn't going to work.

"I don't suppose we have other cops coming in to help?" I asked hopefully. *"There's an army of fae out here."*

"There are armies of fae throughout the city," Chief Carter replied. *"I told them to stay put and keep the people as safe as possible. Of course, the people are fighting back anyway, so who knows how much the PPD is really helping out there?"*

"Got it," I said. *"Well, our plan is only going to help buy you some time. If you have other ideas to clear these fuckers out..."* I stopped and winced. *"Sorry, Chief. Anyway, tear gas or whatever would be good."*

"Already planned, Piper," Pecker replied. *"We've got a number of cadets in the high windows prepping to launch canisters into the crowd right now, in fact."*

"Then we'd better get started," I said, satisfied that we'd

be attacking these guys from multiple positions. *"Let's crack them off, guys."*

I had a feeling that Methkins, Brazen, and Kix were all giggling at my statement. Reaper wouldn't, obviously, but that was only because he was too mature for that sort of thing.

"You heard the lady," Brazen said, chuckling. *"Let's crack a few off."*

Yep.

Three fae hit the ground an instant later. They were all sentries, too.

That caught the attention of those closest to them, but before they could react, we placed Death Nails into them as well. This started a chain reaction, though. Fae spun and lifted those automatic weapons that they so sneakily hid. They didn't even bother to pinpoint where our shots had come from. They just started lighting up everything.

So much for moving to a different position.

"I'm hit," Kix called out. *"Leg only, but holy fuck does that hurt."*

"Hang in there," I called back. *"Fire back if you can; otherwise, scoot back and try to hide yourself."*

"I've scanned his position," Reaper replied. *"I can get to him, but it will—"*

"No, don't," Kix interrupted. *"I've still got a couple of healing potion bottles on me."*

"Are you sure they're healing potions?" Brazen asked.

"Shit."

If he accidentally gulped down one of the concoctions of pain, that would reveal his position to the fae because he'd be screaming. They'd make quick work of him at that point.

"Reaper, how close are you to him?" I asked in a direct connection.

"Close, but I don't think I can get there without being spotted."

"Then don't try. We have to take out the fae first, if we can. Keep doing whatever you were planning to do." I didn't wait for his reply before opening to a full connection again. *"All right, Kix, you're going to have to tough it out."*

"I'll be fine," he said, slurring his words a bit. Blood loss was already hitting him, obviously. *"Just need to sleep for a bit."*

"No sleeping, pal," Brazen yelled back. *"We can't do this without you. Now, get your ass moving or drink one of those fucking bottles. I don't know if it's pain instead of healing, but it's worth a fucking shot."*

"Yeah," was all Kix said.

"Pecker, can you transport him in?"

"Not without stopping our fluctuations," he answered, *"and they're getting closer and closer to breaking through already. If we hold up for even a second, we're busted."*

Damn it. I had an officer bleeding out, an army of fae about to bust through, and...

"Reap, can't you just transport straight to Kix?"

"I can try," he said as if just thinking of this for the first time as well. We *were* under a lot of pressure here, after all. *"I'll at least be able to get close."*

"Do it," I commanded. *"Everyone else, start firing like mad."*

We began unleashing round after round into the fae.

They were firing back at us, of course, but we kept plugging away. Their shots weren't as carefully placed because they were all trying to avoid being hit by us. They had the numbers, but we had the advantage of the proverbial 'shooting fish in a barrel.'

"I've got him and am applying healing," Reaper announced. *"He's lost a lot of blood, though."*

I direct connected again. *"Reap, what were you going to do with Meth?"*

"He was drawing up runes to help power me so that I could unleash a large energy pulse, but there wasn't enough time."

I fired off a few more rounds and then ducked back behind a wall.

"Piper, I don't think I can save Kix."

"Well, you have to, Reap," I replied fiercely. *"Either that or find a way to get him inside that building."*

I didn't wait for a response from him. If I knew Reaper as well as I thought I did, he'd find a way. Even if…

Oh, damn.

"I'm giving him the potion," Reaper replied. *"Don't worry about him screaming. I will stun him first."*

Oh, good.

"Smart!"

A few moments later, with projectiles littering the area where I was 'hiding,' Reaper announced that Kix was fully healed. I knew I could count on Reaper to do his job.

"That's great," I said through our standard broadcast. *"Now, we have to figure out how the hell to get through these fae. Where are those fucking canisters, Pecker?"*

"We're trying."

Right then, the *rat-a-tat-tat* sound of gunfire stopped.

Everything stopped. It was like we'd stepped out of a war zone and into a soundless world of peaceful reprieve.

I glanced around the edge of the building and saw that the fae were all staring off to the right. Even those who were focusing on breaking into the precinct were looking up the street.

Slowly, I turned and spotted what they were seeing.

Another army of fae were incoming.

"*You guys seeing this?*" I said with a gulp.

Brazen's was the sole reply.

"*We're fucked.*"

CHAPTER 29

*J*ust as I was about to make peace with my maker—something I neither believed in nor did I truly believe I could make peace with even if I *had* believed in it—the fae at the front of the oncoming army became clear.

"*Uh, guys,*" I said, "*I think that's Minos.*"

"*The dude from the Faeland who let us go?*" asked Methkins.

"*Yeah.*"

"*Remember that they're tricksters, Piper,*" Brazen warned me. "*Don't let them fool you.*"

I looked around at our situation. What difference would it make if Minos and his fae army were fooling us? It wasn't like we were going to survive anyway.

"*I don't think it will matter what their plan is,*" Reaper said, being the voice of reason. "*If they decide to support Temperance, we will fall.*"

"*Canisters are ready, Piper,*" Pecker informed us.

"*No, wait,*" I called back. "*Hold off on that. We may have a supporting army here.*"

Chief Carter chimed in. "*What?*"

I explained the situation to him. He agreed that it would be best to let this play out, but he commanded Pecker and the crew of rookies to be ready at a moment's notice.

Minos stopped not far from my position.

He glanced over at me and nodded.

I nodded back, thinking that he was a guy I could definitely add to my one-night-stand list. Not only because he was hot as hell, but also because he was playing that knight-in-shining-armor card right now. No, I wasn't one of those damsel-in-distress types. In fact, I usually stuck my foot up the ass of any man who treated me that way. But Minos had a certain something that demonstrated he wasn't doing this for *me*, he was doing it because it was the right thing to do.

Call me crazy, but I found that sexy.

"Minos?" Temperance yelled from her position. "You are supposed to be in prison with the other traitors."

"I believe it is *you* who has turned on your fellow fae, Temperance," he replied sharply. "Going in league with that mage has twisted your mind, turning your beauty to nothing but filth and hate."

I glanced over at her.

Nope, she was still one incredibly attractive woman.

Minos must have been talking about her inner beauty or something. Then again, maybe there was a hair out of place that I couldn't spot from here.

"Back off now, Minos," she warned, "or we will destroy every last one of you."

"Is it not your intention to do that anyway, Temperance?" he countered.

She held up her hand and slowly pointed at him.

"I give you my last warning, Minos."

Minos mimicked the hand up and pointing bit. I'd never heard of that before, but I guessed it was a fae thing.

"And I give you mine, Temperance."

With that, all of Minos's people flicked their hands, and weapons appeared out of nowhere. But these weren't the badass guns like Temperance's fae had. These were shiny swords like the ones elves had.

I jolted at that thought. Were fae what the elves were based on? No fuckin' way. They *did* look like them though, minus the pointy ears, anyway.

Temperance began to laugh heartily.

Honestly, I could see her point. The saying that you don't bring a knife to a gunfight was being demonstrated here. But, fortunately, Minos wasn't stupid.

He snapped his fingers again.

Those swords flashed and turned into guns that were just as fancy as the ones Temperance's gang carried.

Her laughter stopped.

Tricksters, indeed!

"*Chief,*" I said, "*I think you may want to pull everyone away from the windows. It's going to get messy out here.*"

I wasn't suggesting it because I thought the carnage may be too much for the rookies to deal with, though it probably was. My point was to make sure that nobody got shot while hanging out and watching the show.

"Already done, Piper."

A warrior's cry launched from Minos, making my girl parts tingle uncontrollably. Oh yeah, he was totally one-night-stand-list-worthy. I highly doubted he'd feel the same about me, being that I wasn't a fae, but a girl could dream.

But now wasn't the time for fantasies.

"Let's help them out, boys!" I yelled through the connector as I stepped out and began firing at Temperance's mob.

My primary concern was making sure I only hit the bad fae. Maybe they could tell who was good and who was bad, but I couldn't, so I just fired at the back of the crowd and hoped for the best.

CHAPTER 30

*W*ith all that firepower, it hadn't taken long to build up a mass of casualties. If it had continued, there'd have been barely any fae left standing.

But Minos did something that I hadn't expected. He charged right into the fray and slammed directly into Temperance, knocking her on her ass.

The two began fighting like a couple of crazed demons.

That resulted in all weapons being stowed away on both sides while hand-to-hand combat took over. It seemed rather stupid to me, but it was definitely less murdery… sort of.

Fists flew, kicks landed, and throws launched.

My adrenaline was driving me to join in and grab the nearest fae for a bit of face smashing. But something told me that the only fight that really mattered was between Minos and Temperance. She was the key to all of this. If she beat him, there'd be no stopping her.

Just as I was about to run in, Reaper called out, *"Stand back."*

I halted a millisecond before a massive wave of energy rolled from about a block down from me. It knocked every fae out there on their asses, except for Temperance.

She merely appeared to grow stronger.

"Didn't expect that," Reaper admitted.

But I did.

She was simply too powerful to be taken down by an energy pulse. We needed to use something a little more pointed with her.

Without hesitation, I walked straight across the mass of twitching bodies and up the little landing that sat in front of the precinct.

"What do you think *you're* going to do?" she asked with a laugh. "If your reaper can't kill me, *you* have no chance."

"You mean because my Death Nails won't penetrate your shield?"

Her smug look was precious. "Precisely."

"Yeah, well, here's the thing I've learned about shields," I said, leaning in conspiratorially, "they don't work close-range."

Her eyes widened momentarily as the Death Nail burst from my gun. She grabbed her chest and grunted for a few moments.

Then, she began to laugh.

I stood there, confused, until she punched me so hard that I flew off my feet and landed on my back. My gun bounced away.

"Do you think I'm some type of idiot?" she snarled, ripping open her shirt to show that she was wearing a vest. "Of course I know that shields can't stop projectiles at a close distance."

"Ah," I replied, rubbing my jaw.

"Now," she said as she stepped over toward me with menace in her eyes, "it's time for you to die."

"Nah, dude," came a completely unexpected voice. "It's you that's gonna kick it."

We both jerked our heads to the side and saw Methkins standing there. He was holding my gun and he had it pointed right at Temperance's head.

"Now, wait," the fae gasped, holding up her hands, "you don't need to do this."

"She's right," said Reaper as he stepped up. "We can have her prosecuted."

"Yes, yes," Temperance agreed quickly. "That would be the ethical thing to do."

I pushed myself up and went to take my gun back from Methkins, but he was having none of that. His face was hardened and he definitely had some unresolved business to work out.

"Think she'll get the death sentence?" Methkins asked after a moment, though he kept his eyes firmly on Temperance.

"There is no death sentence in the Netherworld, you pathetic little asshole."

Then, she winced.

"Oooh," I breathed. "Shouldn't have said that."

"According to this gun, man, there *is* a death sentence," was the last thing that Temperance heard before a Death Nail entered her skull and she fell over.

"Wow," I said, staring over at Methkins with wide eyes. "Meth, I owe you a fucking hotdog."

CHAPTER 31

*R*eaper and I sat in the chief's office, going over everything that had happened. While technically we weren't able to collect a commission on Temperance, seeing that she wasn't a runner and this wasn't our jurisdiction, Chief Carter still hooked us up with a bonus.

"So Temperance was working with Keller on all of this?" asked the chief.

"Yep," I replied. "We saw her talking to him when we ended up in a dimensional box. But it turns out that he turned his back on her and left her to clean up the mess."

"Because he just wanted to sow seeds of discord," the chief mused.

Had the chief started playing *World of Warcraft* or Dungeons & Dragons or something lately? I mean, who uses 'seeds of discord' in a sentence, except for people who fiddle around in games like that?

Methkins, probably.

Which reminded me…

"Listen," I said, not believing what was about to come out of my mouth, "I think that Meth has turned a corner."

"Meth?" said the chief.

"She's speaking about the wizard, Mr. Methkins," explained Reaper.

"Ah, right. Go on."

"Well, whatever happened to him down there changed the guy. I don't know if it had to do with the electricity or having his fingers smashed or..." I shrugged. "That sick fae did a lot of crazy shi...stuff to us, Chief."

He nodded tightly. "I'm sorry for that."

"It *did* suck," I muttered.

Reaper glanced away.

"Anyway, I think that maybe Meth has a chance to make something of himself." Seriously, that was *not* easy for me to say. "He just needs to have a purpose and the right people to watch over him."

The chief pushed around one of the papers on his desk and then looked up at me.

"Is that your way of volunteering, Piper?"

"Me?" I choked. "Oh, hell no. I was just trying to—"

"Because it really sounded like you were volunteering."

Reaper was smiling now.

"Son of a bitch," I hissed, and this time I did *not* apologize.

We all sat there in silence for a minute. It had been one hell of a day, and it was going to take a while to process everything.

"My worry," the chief said, "is that Keller has succeeded in weakening us even further. We can't stand another rout because of him."

"But we have the people on our side," Reaper pointed out, "especially once it becomes clear how all of these riots happened. They will put aside their differences and fight a common enemy."

"You've still got a lot to learn about people, Officer Payne," the chief sighed. "And even if they are willing to work together, which I highly doubt, who knows how many of them are already infected with Keller's teachings?" He grabbed for another bottle of pink liquid. "For all we know, there could be agents inside here who have fallen under his spell."

That was a sobering thought.

Anyone in here would be able to open the gate for the evil mage.

"Shit," I said.

"I couldn't have said it better myself," the chief agreed with a nod.

CHAPTER 32

It was time to eat crow. I didn't want to, of course, but what choice did I have? That damn turtle had done a bang-up job today.

"Reaper," I said as I stood before him, Brazen, Kix, Methkins, Pecker, and Agnes, "would you please tell Agnes that I appreciated her help today?"

"You just told her yourself," Reaper replied happily. "She can hear you just fine, Piper. You just can't hear her."

"Right."

"Oh," he added, "and she says, 'Nada problem.'"

"Nada problem?"

"It's how she speaks," he answered with a shrug.

I had to believe that, seeing as it was definitely *not* how Reaper Payne spoke.

"Anyway," I said, crossing my arms as I stood in front of them, "it looks like we're the go-to team for dealing with Keller. I don't know if it's because he failed to kill me as a child—" I pointed at Brazen as he opened his mouth.

JOHN P. LOGSDON & CHRISTOPHER P. YOUNG

"Before you think to call me Piper Potter or something similar, I suggest that you remember I hold your career in my hands."

He closed his mouth.

Reaper, Pecker, and Methkins started to giggle.

I gave them a concerned look. "What?"

"Nothing, nothing," Pecker said, wiping his nose. "You were saying?"

"What?" I repeated more firmly.

Reaper chuckled again and said, "It's just that Agnes suggested a better name for you would be 'Harry Piper.'"

The others laughed.

I gave the turtle a dark look.

She didn't seem bothered.

"Hilarious," I said, quieting them down. "Can we get back to discussing the fate of the world now, please?"

It took a few more seconds for them to chill.

"Wait," I said to Methkins as a slap of realization hit me, "*you* can hear her, too?"

"Yeah, man. Why?"

"What about you two?" I asked Brazen and Kix.

They shook their heads. Maybe it was a magic thing?

No, that couldn't be it.

It would mean that Pecker was magical.

Yes, I recognized how wrong that sounded.

"Whatever," I grunted, waving my hands to void that image from my mind. "Anyway, the chief has suggested that we may be facing a full-scale attack soon against the station, but this time it'll be coming from topside."

"How's that possible?" asked Kix. "Pecker's changed the codes on everything."

"Which won't matter if there's a mole," Pecker replied. I gave him an appraising glance. He gave me a look and added, "I've been worried about that since all this started."

"Any suggestions on how to counter it?" asked Reaper.

"Yeah," he replied, "but I can't tell you about them."

We all understood that. If any one of us had been tampered with by Keller, Pecker divulging the info would make it impossible to know which of us cracked. I knew it wasn't me, and I was damn sure it wasn't Reaper.

But what about the others?

I glanced at Agnes.

She *was* a talking turtle, after all. But wouldn't Reaper have sensed something strange?

Then I looked over at Methkins.

He'd been nothing but a stoner up until he ended up in that box. What if Keller and Temperance had gotten to him in that building before the guards had dragged him across the field for torture?

I bit my lip at the prospect.

No, that couldn't be it. Why would they have tortured him at all, if they wanted him on their side? Plus, he was the one who killed Temperance. But then again, that could have been Keller's plan.

Could it be they knew that Reaper and I were coming after him?

They sure didn't seem to know, but the fae *were* tricksters, right?

Brazen and Kix had also been holed-up down there. They'd spent time in that camp. For all I knew, Keller could have gotten to them, too.

Shit, when I really thought about it, *all of them* could be held as suspect.

That was the problem with dickheads like Keller, he sowed seeds of discord.

I couldn't believe I just thought those very words.

"All right," I groaned, "we'll have to be on our toes at all times."

Nobody said anything.

~

"I know it's unlikely that anyone on our immediate crew is in league with Keller, Reap," I said, knowing full well that Agnes could hear me, "but we have to be careful."

"I was thinking the same thing earlier," he replied.

The tube was coming to a stop in the Diamond District and he got up.

"Any interest in having dinner with me and Agnes?" he asked. "We were thinking about freeze-dried shrimp and leafy greens for her and a nice salad for me."

"Sounds dreadful," I said, feeling anxious about admitting it, "but I'm doing dinner with Minos."

He raised an eyebrow at me and nodded.

"Interesting," he said.

"Yeah, yeah, yeah," I replied, knowing damn well I was blushing.

"Good night, Piper."

"G'nite, Reap."

As the tube pulled from the station, I couldn't help but think that there was going to be more trouble hitting us soon.

Keller had us right where he wanted us.

I could only hope he'd hold off for tonight, because I seriously wanted to grab Minos and jump his bones.

～

The End

～

Thanks for Reading

If you enjoyed this book, would you please leave a review at the site you purchased it from? It doesn't have to be a book report... just a line or two would be fantastic and it would really help us out!

John P. Logsdon
www.JohnPLogsdon.com

John was raised in the MD/VA/DC area. Growing up, John had a steady interest in writing stories, playing music, and tinkering with computers. He spent over 20 years working in the video games industry where he acted as designer, programmer, and producer on many online games. He's now a full-time comedy author focusing on urban fantasy, science fiction, fantasy, Arthurian, and GameLit. His books are racy, crazy, contain adult themes and language, are filled with innuendo, and are loaded with snark. His motto is that he writes stories for mature adults who harbor seriously immature thoughts.

Christopher P. Young

Chris grew up in the Maryland suburbs. He spent the majority of his childhood reading and writing science fiction and learning the craft of storytelling. He worked as a designer and producer in the video games industry for a number of years as well as working in technology and admin services. He enjoys writing both serious and comedic science fiction and fantasy. Chris lives with his wife and an ever-growing population of critters.

CRIMSON MYTH PRESS

Crimson Myth Press offers more books by this author as well as books from a few other hand-picked authors. From science fiction & fantasy to adventure & mystery, we bring the best stories for adults and kids alike.

www.CrimsonMyth.com